WHEN PUSH COMES TO SHOVE

A NOVEL

BONITA FABIAN

*Dedicated to David, Kelli, Brad, Jenna, EmilyRose, Caitlin
and my three grandsons.*

ISBN 978-1-66782-106-1 (Print)
ISBN 978-1-66782-107-8 (eBook)

CONTENTS

PROLOGUE

She fell so gracefully, her white chiffon dress billowing outwards like a puffy white cloud and when her body hit the freshly mowed lawn there wasn't a thud, or a thump, just complete silence. She lay sprawled elegantly, as if posing for a photoshoot, without a single drop of blood. None of us knew how to behave, we didn't know the etiquette when someone falls to their death. Do we stay and stare? Do we rush downstairs? Or do we take another sip of champagne and wait for the paramedics to arrive? Most of us did just that.

past her as if she was a stranger. She trotted breathlessly behind me like a worn-out mare as I sprinted ahead towards home.

She was self-conscious of her lumpy body, yet she wore figure hugging clothes that accentuated every roll.

"Do you prefer a real woman like me with curves or a bony emaciated girl like the runway models?" she asked my father.

"How many times must I tell you that I like something to hold on to?" he said.

"So, you like me fat?" she said.

"Exactly," he answered.

"So now you're calling me fat?" she said.

"You are not fat!" He said, "maybe chunky but then as I've said before, I am a chubby chaser."

I don't remember one day of my childhood that my mother wasn't on a diet. I must give her credit for her persistence and renewed hope of every diet known to mankind. As each one failed, she was convinced that the next one would be the holy grail of weight loss. She ate cabbage soup for two weeks, or only boiled potatoes for a month, she would lose some weight only to regain it back very fast. She was always hungry; her nerves were shot, and she was irritable. Then she would be mad at herself if she succumbed to her chocolate craving after consuming an entire box of Sees, become remorseful and cry. The worst part for me was that because of her unhealthy relationship with food, she was a bad cook and had little enthusiasm to cook for the family when she couldn't eat any of it. My father finally resorted to buying frozen dinners for the family which we would choose whichever we wanted to heat them up in the microwave.

My mother who claimed that she did not want to draw attention to herself, dressed in attention-seeking outfits. She was partial to wearing animal prints—her favorite outfit was a figure-hugging leopard print dress, bright red platform high heels with a floppy red hat. She had a pretty face with big blue eyes that always looked startled as if she was always expecting a disaster to happen.

"Do I look good?" she asked my father.

"Someone will call the zoo asking if a leopard escaped," he said laughing.

One Sunday morning while walking back from the corner store with my fifth-grade crush Kerry, I spotted my mother getting off the bus in a zebra coat and matching handbag. I snuck right past her, stopping at a random parked Mercedes Benz, opened the front passenger seat, slid inside leaving Kerry startled on the sidewalk.

My mother approached speedily, "What are you doing?" she said, "get out of that car this instant! What is wrong with you?"

She pulled me home by my ear.

If it is true that opposites attract, then my parents were a perfect example.

My mother was an exotic creature and my father a giant teddy bear. Always upbeat and jolly, smiling to all and sundry. Strangers would ask me, "Are you Grant Selig's son? What a great guy!"

He was not the stereotypical Chartered Accountant boring perfectionist numbers guy, but a gregarious man with a good sense of humor who charmed a large loyal clientele.

No one was a stranger to him—he had a gift that made people feel as if they were the only person in the room, which annoyed my mother when his attention was riveted on a pretty female. People felt that they could confide in him, even random strangers would tell him their most shockingly personal secrets. These confessionals could take place even when our family were in hearing distance, sitting in a restaurant, his food would be getting cold while the manager told him about his messy divorce. We all got to hear the details how he caught his wife having sex in the shower with the gardener.

My father enjoyed being on committees, he was on the town council, president of the Better Business Bureau and a boy scout leader even though none of us were in the scouts. While everybody adored my father, my mother was not as popular; she had a reputation of being a bitch. She was adamant to tell it like it is and it was from her that I learned to never do that. She had strong opinions on everything and everybody and as a result no one liked her. That's when I knew that if I wanted to be popular and liked, I had to be fake like my father.

He was much quieter at home; detached from the family because he had exhausted all his niceties with the general public.

Everyone in my family is short and compact except for me—I am tall and thin. At fifteen my older sister, Lisa had a butt that took up most of the sofa, my younger brother Adam's ass was developing in that direction, so I ended having to watch TV from the floor. My mother did not learn her cooking from The School of Gourmet, but rather from recipes on the back of the boxes of Rice-a-Roni, Hamburger Helper and Hormel. A dinner staple was spaghetti, topped with a can of cream and mushroom Campbells' soup, one pot chili for Sunday lunch, potato and corn chowder and our all-time favorite, beef tacos from a store-bought kit. I had always tolerated my mother's cooking which was better than the frozen meals, until I walked into the Barrett's house and discovered what real food tasted like.

I had been watching Kerry Barrett for a few months until I had the courage to grunt at her. From my second-floor bedroom window, I could see directly into the Barrett's backyard. Kerry would usually be lying in a swing chair reading a book while her brothers played in the pool. They were the only family on our block with a swimming pool so there was stiff competition from the neighborhood kids to befriend them. My younger brother Adam was in second grade with Kerry's brother, so he was the first to be invited over. Then I finagled my way in and my modus operandi to get Kerry to notice me was to be as mean as possible to her. I can't count how many times I pushed her in the swimming pool and made her cry. My constant bullying came to an abrupt halt when Kerry finally had enough and kicked me in the stomach until I threw up. She had thought that I hated her, and although I was mortified I mustered the courage to explain that it was the opposite, I actually liked her. Our parents made us make up, I apologized, and we called it a truce.

The Barrett home was not only a page out of Homes and Garden, but it also smelled of fresh cut flowers and apple pie. The two reasons that I hung out in this white-on-white Nirvana was to check out Kerry, and for the food. Mrs. Barrett took their meals to the next level, she prided herself on being a gourmet cook, she was a graduate of the Cordon Bleu cooking school. I was introduced to dishes that I had never heard of let alone tasted. Grilled Lobster, beef filet, lamb chops, Dover Sole, vichyssoise, roasted artichokes and ethnic foods, like chicken curry and spaghetti ala aglio e olio. I timed my visits close to the dinner hour hoping that I would be invited to stay, and I usually was.

Mr. Barrett had confided in my father, that Kerry and her brother were adopted. Mrs. Barrett was infertile, and they had exhausted all paths to having a child of their own, they then chose adoption which was the best thing that they ever did. My father, of course told my mother and we overheard. The Barretts were the family that I felt I should have belonged to; I became obsessed with wishing that the Barretts would adopt me, yet I couldn't come up with a reason why they should. I wished I was an orphan but until then there was no hope and besides, I don't even think that they really liked me.

Unlike my parents, Mr. and Mrs. Barrett spoke in soft tones to each other, "Yes, darling, I agree," Mrs. Barrett would say to her husband, "adopting Eli would be a good idea, let's call his parents and discuss."

But that would never happen.

The Barretts looked like a Ralph Lauren advertisement. They were always dressed as if they were going boating or on a picnic in a lavender field.

Mr. Barrett wore a cardigan wrapped around his shoulders that whispered, "I am special."

Mrs. Barrett, the children and the family golden retriever, glided in a pearly mist with their upturned noses and cherubic smiles. I walked beside them in my baggy corduroy jeans and checkered shirt purposefully tripping Kerry up with my foot.

"Sweetie, that's not the way to attract butterflies," said my Barrett to me, "you have to act sweet like nectar."

CHAPTER TWO:

HAILE

I t has taken me twenty years of intense therapy to realize that I'm not a tar-
nished, unlovable person and that what happened was not my fault. After all
these years I still cannot grasp the concept of love. I understand the notion of
infatuation, the giddy, heady feeling that you get when you meet someone for
the first time, but I know that never lasts because sooner or later reality steps in
and the flaws you overlooked now stare you in the face. Even couples who have
been together for many years 'settle' because it's easier to stay then to leave. I am
cynical about what love means—a parent's love for their child should be the most
powerful protective love of all and I didn't get that, and I have spent my life trying
to figure out what went wrong.

For the first seven years I thought that my father was the best person in the
whole world. He made me feel safe. To me he had the answers to every question,
everything he said was gospel, even my mother never argued with him. He was
large man whose presence filled the room, and no one dared to mess with him.
My mother was a stay-at-home mom to three children and because my father
made enough money for us to live well, he encouraged her to stay home. There
was nothing that made me happier than sitting on his lap watching nature stories
on Discovery TV. All I wanted was his approval and for him to think that I was
smart. Everything changed when I turned eight and he bought a chess set. He
announced to my mother that he was going to teach me chess because I showed
an aptitude towards cerebral theories. I did not understand what that meant but I
was so proud that he chose me instead of my siblings.

He set up the chess pieces on an antique chess table next to the piano in our
music room. He patiently explained the different pieces and their role and how

they moved. I didn't get the concept right away, but he had the patience to explain it all until I did. He told me that the more I played the easier it would become, and the more I would enjoy the challenge.

One evening when my mother had left for her weekly book club meeting, we set up the game as usual and soon after we began to play, my father did something that shook me to my core. My sister and brother were upstairs in their bedrooms when my father moved his chair closer to mine. He then lifted my hand and placed it on his crotch. I felt something move underneath and I immediately pulled my hand away. What could be moving under his pants? I knew that this was something not right. He picked up my hand and with his hand covering mine he circled the vibrating lump in his pants. His face was red, and he was breathing hard.

I jumped up, "What are you doing?" I said and dashed to my bedroom.

I sat on my bed shaking, I didn't understand what he did but I did understand that this was a bad thing and I felt sick.

The next day he carried on as nothing had happened and never mentioned a word, he made me my favorite hot chocolate and placed it on the table without making eye contact. I began to dread our chess games and when my mother left the house an icy gray fog descended upon me—I knew my father was going to do weird things to me. After the rubbing over his pants, he now progressed to reaching inside of my pajamas and massaging my privates with his fingers, I pulled his hand away, but he fought me.

I jumped up shouting, "Stop it!"

He told me to keep quiet. He said, this is what fathers do to their favorite child and I should be honored that he loved me so much. He went on to explain in a monotone voice that true love is special and hard to find—he picked me because he felt a bond stronger with me than my sister and brother.

My nights turned into horror; my bedroom was not a safe place any longer. He started coming into my room late at night after everyone including my mother were asleep. I pretended that I was sleeping, and I just let him do whatever he wanted while I kept my eyes shut tight. Sometimes I opened them and looked up at the ceiling fans illuminated by the light of the moon and pretended that I was flying on the whirling blades as a superhero saving the world from evil.

In the beginning I asked him, "Does Mommy know?"

He said that if I told anyone, the family would be destroyed. My mother would divorce him, and we would be taken away and put in foster care. He said some people don't understand the true love of a father for his child and because of that our family would be broken apart.

"Do other people do this?" I asked.

"Yes, but only if they love their children too much. This is our secret, and no one must ever know," he said.

"This is our secret," he told me, "No one must ever know."

For Spring break my parents surprised us with a seven-day cruise to the Caribbean Islands. My father started a new job in administration at the head office of Caribbean Cruise Shipping in Miami. We had never been on a cruise before and one of the perks of his job was an annual all expenses paid cruise for employees and their families. The cruise was a round trip from Miami to the Eastern Caribbean islands. The port of Miami was a short drive from our house, and we were picked up by a driver in a large black van to take us there. The ship was newly built and very impressive, we had two adjoining cabins with balconies—one for my parents and little brother, and the other for me and my sister. As soon as the boat left the dock and after the boring muster drill, my mother went up to the Kids Club on the top deck to sign us up for the daily activities. I didn't have any intention of going but to keep the peace I just went along with it. My sister and I were in the same group and Adam in the toddler one.

We had seven days of independence from our parents, they told us that we were free to do our own thing in the day, but the one rule was to meet up for dinner with the family each night. After the first day at sea our first stop was on the island of St. Martin. My father arranged for a taxi to drive us from the Dutch side where we were docked, over the mountain to the French side. The taxi dropped us off at Orient Bay and we spent the day floating in the clear turquoise water. We then had a seafood lunch at an outdoor restaurant on the beach. I had never seen my mother so happy, she was giddy with joy, and with her slicked back wet hair and sun-tanned skin, she looked the prettiest I had ever seen her. Even my father was in a good mood, he allowed us to order anything from the menu, and a Coca Cola which was a big treat.

By the time we got to the island of St. Thomas everything had changed. We had gone off the boat and took a short cab ride to the town of Charlotte Amalie where my mother was looking to buy a new watch to take advantage of the duty-free shopping. It was very hot, and we all were becoming impatient with going in and out of every jewelry store comparing styles and prices.

My father said, "Are you kids getting hot and thirsty?"

My sister and I said that we were, my brother was asleep in the stroller.

"OK, we are going back to the ship," he said to my mother, "this is too hot for the children."

He grabbed me by my hand and started walking towards the taxi stand.

"What about me?" said my sister.

"She needs a new bathing suit," said my father to my mother, "after you find your watch, get her a bathing suit and put it on the Amex."

Before she could answer my father marched us off to get a cab back to the boat.

When we went up the gangway and punched our ID cards in at the security stand, I looked at the ship's security guard wanting to ask for help, but no words came out of my mouth. My father took me to my cabin and shut the door.

"You are a mess," he said, "covered in sand, get into the shower."

He turned on the water, told me to take my clothes off and pushed me in. He came in too. He soaped my body down, then he soaped his body down, then he made me go under the shower and told me to bend down. I was screaming from the searing pain, and he put his hand over my mouth. When it was over, he led me out and gently dried me off. He wrapped a towel around me and held me sobbing in his arms.

"I know you don't understand, but I love you," he said.

He went to his cabin through the inter-leading door, and I lay on my bed curled up in a ball,

I don't know how long I lay there but soon my mother was banging on the wall.

"Get dressed for dinner, hurry up! We will meet you in the dining room."

When I walked in to the dining room and approached the table, she said, "Stand up tall, your posture is so bad. We take you on a wonderful cruise and all you do is look miserable."

"Honey, leave it alone," said my father.

"Look at the beautiful watch that Daddy bought me," she said holding up her wrist and flashing it around the table.

I never went back to the Kids Club, I spent the days in the pool alone, or in the library reading a book. The best thing on the cruise was the soft serve ice cream machine on the pool deck. A successful day was how many cones I would manage to eat. I was sitting on the low wall that circled the swimming the pool licking an ice cream cone when I noticed a boy about my age also eating an ice cream. I turned to face him as he was licking melted drops off his wrist.

He spoke first "Why are you crying?" he said.

"I'm not crying," I said, "I have something in my eye."

"You have snot running down your nose," he said.

I wiped my nose with the back of my hand.

"I saw you at the Kids Zone the first night," he said.

"It's lame," I said, "boring."

"Well, what else is there to do on this ship?" he said. "It's pizza night tonight you should come."

"I'll see," I said.

"Do you like the cruise?" he said.

"It sucks, big time."

He shrugged his shoulders and we both finished our ice creams in silence.

My mother came by from lunch, "I thought I'd find you here," she said. "You should go back to the cabin for a nap."

"Mom, I don't need a nap, I'm not an old person like you," I said as she walked away.

I got up to leave.

"See ya," the boy said.

"What's your name?" I asked.

"Eli."

I plucked up the courage to go up to the top floor to the Kids Zone and as soon as I walked in, I saw Eli and walked towards him.

"At least you're not crying," he said.

He was playing a video game. I sat down at the machine next to his and started playing.

"I'm useless at this," I said.

Soon two kids stood beside me watching me make a fool of myself, so I got up and walked away.

Eli brought me a slice of cheese pizza on a paper plate, and we sat next to each other.

"Let's go swimming," someone yelled.

The counselors said that no one could leave without a parent's signature. Most of the parents came up right after they were called and signed their children out, only me, my sister and Eli remained.

"My parents are too mean to come and get me early," he said.

"Mine are probably drunk," I said.

"Mine are probably drunk and having sex," he said.

"I hate mine," I said.

"Me too." He said, "Sometimes."

We snickered, high-fived and I felt better.

Later that night my parents had a big argument, we could hear them yelling through the cabin walls.

"Why did you have to fucking flirt with the bartender all night?" said my father.

"Oh, nonsense," she said, "It was just innocent fun."

"You asked him to meet you up on the deck later," he yelled, "did you think that I wouldn't hear?"

"I was just kidding," she said, "you just can't stand if any man finds me attractive."

"If anyone wants you, they can have you," he said.

After the cruise my life was divided in nights and days. In the day everything appeared normal, I went to school, had piano lessons, interacted with my friends while trying to keep dark thoughts from creeping in my mind. My mother

Janna was already there when I walked in, sitting at the bar sipping a dirty martini. The first thing I noticed were her breasts spilling out of her low-cut blouse, the second thing I noticed was her lovely smile.

"Well, hello there Mr. Selig," she said. "You have to try the truffle butter popcorn, it's addictive," she said pushing the aluminum bowl towards me.

I sat down on the empty bar stool beside her and ordered a scotch on the rocks.

"So, what's happening?" I said.

"Same old—very busy, I just closed on a four bedroom at The Estates at Aqualina."

"Congratulations, that's awesome," I said, "I think they have a winner there—Karl Lagerfield did an amazing job with the interior just before he unfortunately passed away."

"I think I'm going to take a few days off and head to St. Barths for some R&R," she said, "before I leave, I want to take my client to see the floor plans at The Ritz."

"Cool," I said, "Would you like me to come with you?"

"I would appreciate it, seeing that's it's your listing," she said taking a sip of her martini, "so how is life, anyone special in it?"

"Zip, zero," I laughed, "single suits me fine for now."

I was surprised that she brought this up, so I changed the subject.

"Why don't we order some bar bites?" I suggested, and she agreed.

Janna was a striking woman; I could see that she was getting a lot of attention from the men seated around the bar. She was hard for me to read; I couldn't tell if she was genuine or fake. I had often seen her around town with a date, yet she was still single and in her early forties, it could mean two things—she didn't want a partner, or a partner didn't want her.

After her second cocktail Janna's eyes were bright and her face flushed, she lifted my hand and started circling my wrist with her fingers, "Love your watch," she said, "what is it?"

"Ulysse Nardin," I said.

"Its very sexy," she said, "like you."

I pretended I didn't hear that and fortunately the food arrived as if on cue. As we were eating, I felt her leg lightly rubbing against mine, I found her flirtation to be disconcerting and I moved my leg away. As soon as we had finished eating, I asked for the check.

"Does that mean no dessert?" she asked with feigned surprise.

"You can absolutely have whatever you like," I said, "I just thought we have an early morning tomorrow."

"I was only kidding," she said, "I hope there will be many other opportunities for us to have dessert."

"What time tomorrow?" I asked.

"Around 9:00 a.m.?"

"Perfect," I said.

We walked out together to the valet stand and waited for our cars in silence. I didn't want to start any kind of relationship with someone whom I was thinking of bringing on board my team.

It was never a good idea to mix business with pleasure, if Janna wasn't the right fit for the company, it would be difficult to let her go if a personal relationship ensued besides, I wasn't attracted to her in that way. I hoped that her coming on so strong to me was the result of too much alcohol and not because she thought by getting into my pants, she would gain an entree into my business.

"If you could wish for one thing now, what would it be?" he asked.

"I guess I could say that I wish for eternal serenity and to be one with the earth but honestly all I wish for is to give you a blow job."

He burst out laughing mussed the top of my hair and said, "Who can say no to that?"

I led him to my bedroom and sat him down on the chaise longue across from my bed. We deep kissed for a while before I undid his slacks.

I looked up at him, he looked like a deer caught in the headlight, his eyes wide open in what I read was panic.

I gave it my best shot, I really tried, but he did not get hard. I felt awkward, this had never happened with me before.

"I'm just really tired," Eli said, "I'm sorry, it's not you, its me."

He looked more resigned than embarrassed—he zipped up his pants and left without a word.

CHAPTER SEVEN:

ELI

I was disappointed in myself; I went ahead and did exactly what I didn't want to do. I was mortified at my weakness, and I refused to blame the alcohol, why did I think that this time things would be different? When I got back home Haile was waiting up for me.

"Why are you up?" I asked.

"I couldn't sleep until I knew you were home safe and sound. Did you have a good night?" she asked.

"I wouldn't call it a good night, but I asked Janna to join Selig and we clinched the deal."

"Was there sex involved?"

"I fucked up as usual," I said, "made an idiot of myself."

"Don't be so hard on yourself," she said.

"I wish I was hard," I said bitterly, "then there wouldn't be an issue."

"You aren't attracted to her?"

"Even if I was, my penis wouldn't get the message, as you know we've been incommunicado for a very long time."

The next morning, I didn't go to the office because my mother had one of her usual 'attacks'. In the last few years, she could be out shopping or meeting up with a girlfriend for lunch when suddenly she would be overcome with dizziness and feel faint. I got another of these regular calls from her best friend Sadie, that they were at Serafina having lunch at the mall when my mother had shortness of breath and sharp pains in her chest, 911 had been called. The ambulance was taking her to the Aventura Hospital. I raced out the door and headed there. My siblings lived in New York City, so the responsibility of my mother fell on me.

When I arrived at the ER, I was immediately escorted to my mother who was lying in bed, in a small cubicle, hooked up to an IV. I was surprised to see that she was texting—my phone pinged, and her texts came through.

"I had a heart attack; can you believe it?" she texted.

The nurse followed me in and said that the doctor will come and talk to me shortly.

"Mom, you had a heart attack?" I asked, "who told you?"

"The doctor," she said, "the pain was unbelievable, like an elephant sitting on my chest."

When the doctor arrived, he looked stressed and disheveled—I wondered why anyone would choose to be an ER doctor, it had to be the most stressful medical profession. He told me that my mother was having chest pains and although they didn't see anything in the scans, he would have to admit her to the cardiac floor for observation. Out of earshot he told me that looking at her prior records he saw that she was a frequent patient to the ER with the same complaint, and this is probably another anxiety attack but they had to make sure.

"Where is Jack?" I asked my mother.

"At the Hard Rock playing blackjack, a game after his name," she said, "I've tried to get hold of him, but his phone must be turned off."

After my father passed away, my mother met Jack on a cruise, and they married soon after. They both came into the marriage with money and a tight prenuptial, so I wasn't concerned that he was gambling my mother's money away. Apart from spending vast sums of money for gambling, Jack was in fact quite frugal. His other hobby was hunting down the lowest price of fruit and vegetables in town. As a retired CEO of a large company, he applied his leadership skills now to everyday shopping. There was also a rumor that he stopped at the Asian massage spa on his way home from the grocery store, but he always came home with a bag of vegetables.

I kissed my mother goodbye and told her that she was in good hands.

"You better call your brother and sister and tell them to be on standby in case they need to fly in for my funeral," she said.

"Mom, the doctor told me that you are going to be fine," I said as I left.

"Remember to put—I TOLD YOU SO—on my headstone," she yelled after me.

There was a voice mail from Janna, "I'm taking a client to look at the penthouse at Continuum, hold thumbs! Last night was great—don't sweat the small stuff," she said laughing.

"Fuck off," I said under my breath.

I headed to the construction site in Golden Beach to see how the La Valle project was progressing, it was raining when I got there, and the crew were packing up.

"There's no lightning," I said, "what a bunch of pussies you all are, afraid of getting wet."

Carlos, the foreman gave me the finger when he thought I wasn't looking. Summer in Florida wasn't conducive to construction, there were more storms and hurricane warnings then regular days, but rain or shine it was always sweltering and humid. I didn't want to be hard on the crew, I was appreciative that unlike their work environment, mine were spent in air conditioning. As I was about to drive off, Camilla La Valle pulled up in her baby blue Bentley convertible.

"Whenever I put the roof down it starts raining," she said, "hold on a sec I need to talk to you."

She ran out to my car holding her Hermes Birkin bag over her hair shielding it from the rain.

I opened the front door of my Aston Martin and she slid in.

"I just had my hair extensions done and now they are wet," she said looking in the front mirror. "So, what's the update on the house?" she asked.

"Everything on track," I lied, "the floors go in next week."

"Good. It's so frustrating living in the rental, I hate it," she said, "it's so tacky and the kids don't have a playroom, and the nanny is sleeping in the laundry room."

Then she burst out crying.

"I think James is having an affair," she said, "sorry to burden you, but I have no one else to talk to."

James La Valle was a top hedge fund guy in Florida, and I had built his impressive office building downtown in Brickell and now I was currently building their mansion.

"Are you sure?" I said, "what makes you say that?"

"He has this pattern whenever he is cheating—he thinks I'm an idiot—he gets overly affectionate, wants sex more than usual and starts buying me expensive gifts—well, his secretary buys them."

"Don't jump the gun," I said, "that just means that he loves you."

"I had to drive his car yesterday and in the cup holder was a Starbucks cup with a girl's name written on it," she said.

"Come on Cami that doesn't mean anything," I said.

"And a valet ticket from Aqualina resort?"

"They could have gone for a business lunch, give the guy the benefit of the doubt," I said.

"I actually don't give a fuck," she said, "If he thinks he could get better than me, he can just piss off."

"That's the spirit," I said.

"But I once caught him before and I'm still not over it," she said sniffing. "I have lost all my trust for him. Please Eli don't breathe a word," she said and opened the car to hop out.

We waved goodbye as I drove out onto the long muddy road that was going to be the circular driveway. The house was a contemporary two-story building in natural slate and olive tree wood with floor to ceiling hurricane force windows, it sat very close to the beach on a large lot with enough land for a garden, pool and tennis court. There would be a separate structure for a guest house. A six-car glass encased garage was being built. This was the non-commercial property I was building in the most coveted and swankiest address, Golden Beach. It was a personal favor from me to James La Valle because he was such a lucrative client.

I drove the short distance home looking forward to a quiet evening catching up on Netflix with Haile.

CHAPTER EIGHT:

HAILE

I am an empath, which means that I can feel the vibrations of someone's mood, good or bad. I am like a sponge that absorbs anxiety and negative energy. This can be exhausting; draining all my energy that often I have to leave a social gathering to regroup. For me being an empath is more of a hindrance then a gift—my intuition works full steam ahead in all my waking hours so that is why I prefer my own company. Eli is the complete opposite; he is extrovert and comes across as never having a care in the world. I envy his disposition, if he ever feels depressed, he is a master of covering it up. He can live in the moment and not allow external influences to hinder him, in other words he doesn't give a shit what other people think. I wish I were like that.

We were sitting in the media room eating Haagen-Daz Bourbon Praline Pecan Ice Cream and watching The Crown on Netflix, when security called up from the front desk.

"There's a Janna Cooper asking to come up and deliver something to you."

"Can she leave it at the front desk?" Eli asked.

"She says that it's an important document."

"OK," he said, "send her up."

He turned to me, "Oh crap, I haven't got the energy to handle her, you tell her that I'm in the shower and she can give it to you."

I jumped up, adjusted my silk robe, ran to the bathroom to fix my hair and put on some lip gloss and when the doorbell buzzed, I immediately opened it. She was dressed simply in a plain sweater and skinny jeans with thigh high boots. She wore little makeup, and her hair was tied loosely in a messy bun. I was surprised that Janna looked more like the girl next door than the femme fatale that I had envisioned.

"Oh, hi," she said trying to maintain her composure, "I wanted to give Eli this contract to go over before I sign it."

"He's in the shower," I said, "I am Haile, Eli's sister, nice to meet you."

"I didn't know that Eli had a sister. Can I come in?" she said, "I need to run some things by him."

I could tell that she was very nervous.

"I'll give it to him, and he will call you tomorrow," I said holding out my hand to take the envelope from her.

She hesitated and stood at the door expecting to be invited in and when she saw that it wasn't an option, I could tell that she was thrown. I could see the cog wheels turning in her head; who the fuck does this sister think she is, controlling who comes in and out of his house?

After she left, I wondered why Janna felt entitled stopping by at Eli's without prior consent.

Eli felt the same way. "What a nerve," he said, "pitching up at my place, I bet she did that on purpose to see if anyone else was here."

He glanced over the papers and said that there was nothing of importance that couldn't be dealt with the following day at the office.

We continued watching The Crown but couldn't concentrate, we were thrown, Eli said he may have made a mistake by asking her to join his company.

"Something about her rubs me up the wrong way," he said.

"Excuse the pun, but you let her rub you up the wrong way," I said with a grimace.

"Shut up," he said.

I Googled her and apart from her business profile on LinkedIn, her professional accomplishments and Facebook page, there wasn't any in-depth personal information. I found her address; she lived in Williams Island, Aventura ten minutes across the William Lehman Causeway from us.

She lived in one of the newer expensive buildings which showed that she had money. Williams Island is fancy enclave of condo buildings built on a luxury manmade 'Tropical Island.'

It was set up with swimming pools, restaurants, tennis courts and a spa. The residents have a sense of entitlement especially if they own one of the large yachts docked at the Marina. I have learned from the real estate business that what appears extravagant can be a mirage. Some wealthy people who are hit by recession or hard times guard their secret of lacking funds with their lives, being poor is the worst crime in these circles. If the word got out via the condo board that a resident couldn't afford the monthly maintenance fees, they would be treated like a pariah.

CHAPTER NINE:

JANNA

I was stunned when I went to Eli's apartment. I was not expecting a tall, sultry, blond woman looking like she stepped off a magazine cover to answer the door and though she smiled when she greeted me, her eyes said, "Who the fuck is this and what the fuck is she doing here?"

I was wondering the exact same thing about her, but her casual demeanor and silk bathrobe told me that she was very much at home. I was at first relieved to hear that she was Eli's sister but when she did not let me in, that threw me. I was annoyed that she took it upon herself to monitor who comes in or not. I had my eye on Eli long before he knew that I existed, and I wasn't going to let a territorial sister ruin my plans.

I walked into our offices and went directly into Eli's suite.

"Did you have time to go over the contract that I dropped off?" I asked,

He looked up from his computer screen and pushed his glasses up onto his head.

"Yes, I did. It is pretty straightforward," he added.

"I met your sister last night," I said.

"She told me," he said.

"Does she live with you?" I asked nonchalantly while looking over some papers.

"Yes, she does," he answered abruptly, and I got the message that the subject was closed.

The fact that he looked annoyed only made me more curious, but I dropped the subject. Eli was a closed book as far as his personal life was concerned, and in the little time that I knew him I hadn't learned much about him. All I knew was that he was single, handsome and rich; whether he was available was a mystery.

I had my heart broken only once and it wasn't pretty. The fact that he was older, married and my boss did not deter me. He told me that he was desperately unhappily married, that his wife was a cold, uncaring woman. He said that they slept in separate bedrooms and hadn't had sex for many years—he included the information that she was overweight and had let herself go. I fell in love with the oldest story in the book, a man whose wife didn't understand him, so he was unhappy and unloved.

He promised to leave her so that we could be together, but each time the opportunity arose, he explained that although I was the love of his life, he didn't want to hurt his three teenage children. After five years of broken promises, I gave him an ultimatum—leave her and marry me or I'm out the door. Surprise! He chose her. I was forced to leave my job, move out of the apartment that he had set up for me and pick up the pieces while he blocked all communication. I made a vow to myself, not that I wouldn't have a relationship with a married man, but that I would never fall in love again.

I was cautious how I managed my business clients, most of my buyers were couples, I made sure to include the women in all our conversations so that they wouldn't feel threatened. I dressed elegantly but not provocatively; I didn't want to be a threat to anyone. Many of my female colleagues would dress sexy and play to the husbands, flirting with them in front of their wives. Even the women with self-esteem and pride would get annoyed because it was presumptuous to assume that the men held the purse strings. These realtors had it all wrong, it's the woman who ultimately makes the decision whether to buy or not, and those wives would drop a threatening agent in a second and never return. I played to the wives so that they felt secure—however, if they weren't present and the husband came to my office alone, I would turn on the charm and stroke his ego as much as I could. I was in this business for the sales and nothing else.

I left the office and headed to meet my next clients at the Peninsula Condos. They were a young Colombian couple with a baby on the way and were looking for an apartment that had live-in nanny quarters. The Peninsula was one of the few apartment buildings in Aventura that offered that. The floor plans were some of the largest in the area. I pulled up to the entrance where the couple were waiting for me, they turned to greet me, the husband giving me a once over from head to toe and the heavily pregnant wife glanced over but didn't smile.

We took the elevator to the 12th floor, I unlocked the door and led them into an expansive living area overlooking the bay.

She immediately said, "I don't like the color of the walls."

They were painted a dark gray—"That can be changed very easily," I said, "you can paint it to whatever color you like."

I led them into the kitchen.

"It's how you say?" she said with a thick Latin accent, "look old fashion."

The husband said, "We can remodel, there is lots of space, lots of bedrooms."

We went into the master bedroom.

"Wow, look at that view," he said.

"I don't like the bathroom," she said, "I want more modern."

We walked through the apartment; it was empty, the prior owners had moved out and it was clean and bright.

"This can be the baby's room," the husband said.

"It's too far from our bedroom," she said.

I left them to look around and although I didn't understand Spanish well, I could tell that she didn't like it, and that she didn't like me.

I was used to this scenario, and it didn't bother me, I already knew what the next step would be. They would make a low-ball offer because there was too much to remodel. A few days later I made a follow up call, got their answering machine and never heard back. You win some and you lose some. Some weeks later Eli told me that he sold them a four-million-dollar apartment at the Fendi Chateaux on the beach; I pretended that I didn't care.

The annual company weekend workshop was coming up at the Breakers Resort in Palm Beach, I had seen the invitations on Eli's desk, and I was wondering if he would bring it up and who would be going? In anticipation I had already started planning the getaway because there was no way that I wouldn't be there. I bought myself a black Jason Wu slinky jumpsuit and two La Perla bikinis. I had already made an appointment for a Brazilian wax and to put in hair extensions.

CHAPTER TEN:

ELI

Camilla LaValle asked to see me concerning the new swimming pool—she was not happy how it was progressing. We met at Miami Juice for a quick breakfast, I was expecting James to join us, but he wasn't there.

"I have something to tell you," she said as she sat down at our table for two on the crowded patio overlooking Collins Avenue.

"About the pool?" I asked.

"No, the pool is fine but remember I said that I thought my husband was cheating?" she asked sipping fresh squeezed orange juice, "well, I think I know with who."

"Yeah?"

"Last month for Valentine's Day James took me to Tiffany's at the Aventura Mall to buy me the Elsa Peretti bangle that I asked for. He never comes up with ideas of his own, so I have to tell him exactly what I want.

"Anyway, as we step into the store, a pretty young girl with dark hair pulled up in a bun, wearing a blazer and tight short skirt, approaches us asking if we needed help. She seats us at a glass counter and my husband says that we want to look at the classic Elsa Peretti bone cuff in silver in a size medium for his wife.

"As she leaves to get it from a back room, I see his eyes follow her butt and high heels—I don't say anything because I'm used to that. She returns with the bangle, I try it on, and it fits perfectly.

"I would like to have it engraved," says my husband.

"She takes out a notepad and shows us the different fonts styles—I choose one and then he says 'I would like these words engraved on the inside—To the Love of my Life.'

"While she is writing it down, I get up to look around at the jewelry in the glass cases and I hear her tell him how lucky his wife is to get such a loving message.

"I wish that I had a man who would do that for me," she said.

'I'm sure a woman as pretty as you wouldn't have a problem finding one,' he said.

He then turns to me and says, 'See anything else that you want?'

'Fuck off,' I whisper.

"Long story short, he took her card, and she was going to call him to pick up the bangle when the inscription was ready. So, guess what? A few days later one of my best friends, Lindy, sees them at The Grill near Tiffany's having lunch, and he has the Tiffany bag with my fucking bangle on the chair next to him."

"Look Camilla, I don't know your husband well but maybe he is just a flirt, nothing more," I said, "some men with big egos need to charm every female that they meet. Can you just turn a blind eye and let him do his stupid thing?"

"He fought so hard to get me, he chased me, he wore me down with diamonds and gifts, now seven years later with two kids, he acts like he is too good for me," she said.

I didn't understand why Camilla felt that she could confide in me about the trials and tribulations of her marriage, it put me in an awkward position between both of my clients.

"Look what a beautiful house you are building together! He is putting in such effort and expense, he wouldn't be doing that if he didn't love you?" I said.

"Perhaps you are right Eli, you are so sweet, I bet you wouldn't make a woman's life a misery."

"I am holding my annual appreciation weekend at The Breakers in Palm Beach at the end of this month," I said, "Why don't you and James join me as my guests? It will be fun."

"Really? But what would we be doing at a Real Estate event?"

"I can ask James to give a short talk on investment banking and tie it up with our theme for the weekend."

"That would be great, The Breakers is our favorite resort. Thanks Eli," she said, "you are the best."

CHAPTER ELEVEN

HAILE

Some people are lucky to have a teacher in school who touched their lives without them ever knowing it—I had such an angel, Mrs. Lowenstein. We called her Mrs. L. I always thought of Mrs. L as an elderly grandmother type—she had a no-nonsense salt and pepper short hairstyle, round wire-rimmed glasses, and a non-descript makeup free face. She was my eighth-grade teacher which was the last year of middle school. Looking back, I realize that she could only have been in her forties at that time.

I was an unhappy child, on the outside I put on a show of being extrovert, confident, funny and smart but on the inside, was another story. My life revolved around hoping and praying that my father would not approach me that night.

Mrs. L was my English creative writing teacher, she often gave me an A plus with a positive comment written on my paper with a red ballpoint pen in her neat cursive handwriting. She would say—'excellent perception, well thought out, good composition, Well done!'

One day she stopped at my desk when the class were writing up our home-work and asked me quietly, "Why are you subjects so dark? You are such a good writer, why don't you lighten up and put some humor in your pieces?"

My last essay was titled, "If I ever..."—it was about an alien child who longs to leave its planet and find another life somewhere else. 'If I ever escape these chains, I will float to higher grounds' - was my opening statement.

I said, "I don't know why, it's just thoughts that pop into my mind."

"You write so well but the next project why don't you try putting a lighter spin on things and see how that goes," she said tousling my hair. "I gave you an A," she said, "but with tears in my eyes."

"I have nothing happy to write about," I said with a shrug.

"If you ever want to talk, you can always come see me after school. I'm always in the class for another one or two hours every day," she said.

I nodded as she walked on along the row of desks.

I knew that I could never tell anyone what my father was doing to me—I was very embarrassed, what if no one believed me? What if I was sending my father signals that I wanted this? What if—as my father said—that the Department of Children Services would remove us from our home and put us all in separate foster care? My father told me that if I ever told my mother he would say that I am a lying piece of shit looking for attention. He reminded me of all the lies that I had told over the years, and he was right. I had lied many times—I had drunk my parent's liquor and filled the bottles with water. I had snuck out of the house to meet up with my friends when my parents were asleep. I would spend hours at a small coffee shop doing my homework instead of coming home then lie that I had stayed at school for club meetings. He was right my mother wouldn't believe me.

I was in the debate club, and our team did well in the inter-school debates, in fact we made the finals to compete in state in Orlando, Florida. This was a big accomplishment for our school. I was a good debater but not the best—I had to overcome my shyness and learned to pretend I was someone else. A teammate once told me to picture everyone in the audience pooping then I wouldn't be so intimidated, so I did, and it helped.

When I told my parents about the debate trip to Orlando my father immediately said that he would be a chaperone. My heart sank and I wanted to get out of going.

"Please Dad, I want to be with my friends, please don't come," I begged.

"Excuse me?" he said. "You are so lucky that you have a father who wants to go with you."

I turned to my mother, "Mom can you come instead?"

"You don't want me to go?" he said loudly, "Are you saying that you are ashamed of your dad?"

"I couldn't think of anything worse than being on a bus with twenty kids," said my mother.

"They have enough chaperones," I said, "they don't need more."

"Then why are they sending out these sheets to sign up?" said my father, "I don't want you going to Orlando with a bunch of kids and parents that we don't know, so if you don't want me there, then you can't go."

The very next day I asked Mrs. L if I could come and talk to her after school. She said of course, I can. As soon as the bell rang, I went to her classroom. She was sitting grading papers and eating a sandwich at the same time.

"Pull up a chair beside me," she said. "So, how's your day been?" she asked.

"Mrs. L." I said, "My father wants to chaperone the debate trip to Orlando, and I don't want him to come."

"And why is that?" she asked.

"He has a very short temper, and I don't think he will make a good chaperone. He has no filters and could insult a lot of the kids without him realizing."

"We are begging for more chaperones," she said, "otherwise we can't go, I'm sure your father can control himself for two days."

"Please Mrs. L, I don't want my father to come with us."

"You are being very selfish, it's kind of your father to volunteer, so just handle it," she said.

The bus transporting our debate team was waiting outside the school at dawn, it was a three-hour ride to Orlando. This event was being hosted by Disney and we were staying at a Disney hotel for the two days where the debates would be held—in the hotel conference room.

The sun was just coming up when we pulled up to the parking lot adjacent to the idling bus. Mrs. L and a male teacher were ushering the students into a line and checking off their names on a list. We had to put our backpacks in the luggage compartment beneath the bus. My father was in great form, high fiving everyone including Mrs. L. He wore a Dolphins tracksuit in orange and turquoise and a dolphins cap. I don't know why he thought he had to dress for a football game.

He was in his element.

"This is going to be fun!" he said punching my shoulder lightly.

We climbed into the bus, and I asked my father if he would please sit with the other chaperones.

"Why would I do that?" he asked.

"I want to sit with my friends," I said.

Mrs. L came down the aisle towards us and gave my father a sheet of paper, "These are the names of the kids that you are in charge of," she said.

He took the sheet and checked the names.

"And these are the hotel rooms that you will be responsible for," she added.

He turned to me, "I asked for us to share a room and I'm pleased to see that we are," he said.

"You are going to be in my room?" I said, "I thought I was in the room with some of my debate team."

Suddenly I became hot and clammy, I couldn't hear what my father was saying, it was like he was talking in a muffled voice coming from a faraway place. My body started shaking and I felt so dizzy that the bus started spinning.

I fell over onto the floor and began vomiting all over myself.

"What the hell?" yelled my dad, "pull yourself together."

Mrs. L and Coach Johnson ran towards us and laid me out flat on the floor of the bus. I could see my schoolmates looking down at me in horror. I had pooped all over myself.

Someone called 911 and I was transported by ambulance to the closest hospital. When I came to in the hospital bed, my mother was with me. The bus, I was told later, left as scheduled and my father had to go without me because without him as a chaperone the trip would have been canceled.

I had an IV attached to me arm.

"What happened?" asked my mother pale and shaking.

I couldn't speak.

I stayed there overnight, the ER doctor ordered a brain cats can, blood tests, urine tests, and neurological exams and everything came up negative. The doctor asked my mother if I was an anxious child and had this ever happened before? She said this had never happened before and I was not an anxious child. The doctor said that it could either be a panic attack or I may have eaten something that was off. My mother suggested that it could have been the undercooked chicken that I ate the night before.

The doctor told me to eat a bland diet for the next few days and then he discharged me from the hospital that evening.

"Was anything worrying you about the trip?" my mother asked.

"Only that I didn't want to share a room with Dad."

"That's it? Why didn't you just tell him that?"

"I did," I said, "he wouldn't listen."

"He is such a good dad, so protective of you," she said, "I'll talk to him. He does not get that you are not a baby anymore."

CHAPTER TWELVE:

JANNA

There was so much to prepare for going to The Breakers. Eli sent out e-vites for the upcoming gala, for all the agents, designers, architects, stagers and office staff; there were close to a hundred count. Significant others were not invited unless you were a special guest. I had a list of things to do, in preparation for the weekend, waxing, tanning, hair extensions, manicures, pedicure—this was how I always prepared for a special occasion. I have Botox injections in my face every four months and fillers in my cheeks, chin, lips once a year. In the last few years, I had a nose job because I wasn't happy with my nose, it was too long and now it is short and narrow. I have had breast augmentation, liposuction on my tummy and arms. I run every day and do Pilates three times a week. In my work and social circles this was standard. The woman of Palm Beach have always had their own style—Lily Pulitzer was the uniform when Jackie Kennedy was alive, and it still is popular. Even the female staff at the Breakers wear Lily Pulitzer dresses with Kenneth Jay Lane necklaces and earrings. Night wear is very elegant floor- length flowing dresses showing lots of skin. Palm Beach may be classy but not prissy, sex still makes this town go around.

I drove the hour and fifteen minutes up to the Breakers Resort in my own car, I was hoping that Eli would have offered me a ride but then I realized that he couldn't single one of his agents out. As you turn off the highway into West Palm Beach and drive over the bridge towards the palm treelined street leading into Palm Beach, you feel that you have come into a luxurious bubble. The streets are wide and the architecture is from a page of Henry Flagler's book. Palm Beach is laid back and exudes unpretentious old money.

The entrance to The Breakers is stunning—at the end of the long circular drive, the building appears like an impressive fortress. The valets whisk away your luggage while you check in, the grandeur of the frescoed ceilings immediately transports one to another era. The female reception staff have their hair pulled back into neat buns with bangs swept into a little back flip. These young women are selected for their looks as well as their efficiency. The male counterparts are dressed in formal suits with crisp white shirts.

I check into my room and am pleasantly surprised to have been upgraded to a large seafront suite. There is a welcome basket from the Selig organization filled with fruits, snacks, Tylenol, sunscreen and flip flops.

I change into my robe and decide to take a brief nap before getting dressed for cocktails at 6.00 p.m. I lie on my back trying not to smudge my makeup that was done earlier in the morning by the Glam Squad who came to my apartment to do my face and hair. I was planning to wear my black backless jumpsuit with black Christian Louboutin shoes.

My phone buzzed, it was Amy from the office, "Hi, Jan, welcome to Palm Beach. Are you settling in? If there is anything that you need, give me a call. I'm in room 546."

"Hi Amy, what is on the tab and what is not?" I asked.

"Everything," she said, "room service, alcohol, mini bar all included for the weekend until Sunday check out. Only Spa services are your responsibility."

"Have the others arrived yet?" I said, "is Eli here?"

"Most everyone has checked in and Eli has been here since midday."

I texted him to say that I had arrived; he immediately texted back that he will see me downstairs at HMF for cocktails and that dinner was going to be held in the Venetian Ballrooms.

I waited fifteen minutes before I went down for cocktails so that I would not be the first to arrive. The HMF bar was in the dazzling Florentine Room which was Palm Beach's hottest gathering place; a roped off area was exclusive for our party.

I had been there many times with my girlfriends hoping to catch one of the hot men congregated around the bar. There were a lot of couples, young sexy women with gray haired older men. Just as the women wore an array of slinky clothes the men had a signature look too. Patterned shirts with contrast rolled up sleeves over fitted pants and soft leather moccasin shoes without socks. An expensive watch—nothing as gaudy as a gold Rolex but a smooth Patek Philippe instead.

I walked into the bar and saw Eli walking towards me, he gave me a big hug.

"You look wonderful," he said, "come and say hi to everyone."

He walked with me in the direction where our group was congregated but he was waylaid by people greeting him along the way, so I stood alone checking out the scene.

A waiter came by with a tray of cocktails and I picked up a glass of white wine. I recognized faces but couldn't put names to most of them. I was new to the group, and I still wasn't fully accepted into the circle. As I approached closer to where the DJ was spinning lounge music the noise level made it difficult to listen to the conversations around me. There was a lot of nodding, prodding, laughter and meaningless dialogue. Soon we all were ushered out of the room and led to the ballroom where dinner was to be served.

I looked at the board with the seating plans and was pleased to see that I was seated at Eli's table. This was the prime table, and I was happy to be included.

The banquet hall overlooking the ocean was breathtaking, twenty tables were set in white linens, each with tall glass vases with cream and lilac baby roses. Twinkling fairy lights lit up the entire room, it looked like a magical wonderland.

I found my name card and sat down next to a handsome tanned man with impossibly white teeth, next to him sat a petite bleached blond woman equally tanned with piercing blues eyes. She checked me out from top to bottom with lightning speed. They introduced themselves as James and Camilla LaValle. Eli's name card was to my left and the other seated couples were strangers to me. When Eli sat down, I asked him softly who the LaValles were and he explained that he was building their estate in Golden Beach and that James was giving the keynote talk the following day.

Throughout dinner I tried to engage with them, James was distracted and his wife, although warm and friendly to everyone else, was cool towards me. When Camilla LaValle left the table to go to the ladies' room, her husband imme-diately turned towards me,

"I didn't get your name?' he said.

"Marianna," I said, "but my friends call me Janna."

"How are you involved with the real estate industry?" he asked with a smile.

"I work with Eli," I said, "I'm in sales."

"Eli is building our new home; you must stop by with him one day and check out the progress."

"Thanks," I said, "I will. I hear it's an amazing project."

He gave me his business card before his wife walked back to the table and for the rest of the evening, he ignored me.

At the end of the evening I turned to Eli, "Would you like to have a night cap out on the terrace?" I asked.

"Not tonight," he said, "we have a long day tomorrow and I'm exhausted."

I was confused by the mixed messages that I got from Eli. He was a friendly person to everyone but there were signs that he seemed interested in me. He would seek me out in a crowd, make conversation or a joke, touch my arm when he spoke to me and sometimes would put his arm around me when we walked. Yet, he never took the opportunity to be with me alone and this surprised me. The Breakers would be the ideal opportunity to be with me if he wanted to, because no one would be the wiser. Perhaps he was embarrassed by the incident that happened at his apartment, when our little tryst ended with a fizzle.

The following day after breakfast in the opulent and beautiful Circle Room, we headed to the seminar in the ballroom. James LaValle was the keynote speaker of the day. He gave a synopsis of how he grew his wealth, investing portfolio from buying property in the Miami area. He was a compelling man—almost too good looking and too confident—the kind of man that would be trouble to get involved with. Camilla was not paying attention to her husband's speech. She seemed bored listening to a familiar story, she was checking her manicured nails and held out her right hand to inspect her huge canary diamond, angling her fingers towards the incoming sunlight entranced by the sparkle. I wondered if she was thinking if that made her marriage worth it.

She looked up and saw me checking her out, and gave me a dirty side look. I enjoyed playing games with wives, I knew that I had the power to make them feel uncomfortable and I got a kick out of it. Women didn't like me, but men did and that's what I really cared about.

CHAPTER THIRTEEN

ELI

The seminar at The Breakers was a big success, not only did the team gain new knowledge, but it was also a good bonding experience, there was a good balance between work and play which I had hoped for. I gave myself a pat on the back for organizing a seamlessly pleasant weekend without any drama. I had some issues with Janna who was pursuing me and therefore putting me in an awkward position. The last night of the seminar, I was sitting with James and Camilla at the Seafood Bar when she walked into the room. She looked stunning in a silver mini dress showing her ample cleavage and she strutted towards us knowing that all eyes were on her. She put her arms around my shoulders and leaned in for a kiss. Her behavior was too familiar for me as her boss, but I let it go. Cami froze immediately, and James didn't pay her any attention. Camilla immediately got up and said that she was tired and going up to bed, James followed her. Janna suggested that we go up to her room for a night cap.

"Umm… I think I have had enough to drink for one night," I said.

"Come on, don't be an old man," she said, "the night is still young."

We took the elevator up to her suite, and as we walked in the door, she unzipped her short dress and stepped out of it leaving it in a pile on the floor. She was totally naked. She came towards me, wrapped her arms around my neck and on tippy toes kissed me. I responded and kissed her back.

Pulling me back onto the bed she commanded that I take my clothes off. I quickly jumped up like cold water had been thrown at my face.

"What's wrong?" she said, "aren't you attracted to me."

"Of course, I am, Janna," I said.

"Then what's the problem?" she asked.

"I don't think that we should be doing this, it's not a good idea."

"Is there someone else?" she said.

"No," I said, "not at all."

"I don't get you Eli. If you aren't involved with anyone then what's your problem? I'm not asking for a commitment for God's sake. Can't we just have a bit of fun?"

I took a few steps backwards, adjusted my clothes and said, "Janna, we work together, it would be unethical to take our friendship further."

She looked at me in disbelief, almost in shock, and I saw a flash of anger in her eyes as I turned and left the room.

I was driving back to Miami listening to music, feeling very down when my phone rang—it was James LaValle.

"Hey, Bro, you put on a sick weekend," he said.

"Thanks man, you blew them away with your talk," I said.

"Who was the hot chick at our table?" he asked.

"Your wife?" I said.

"She too," he said, "but the hot dark hair chick with the transparent blouse and awesome boobs."

"That's my colleague, Janna Cooper," I said, "She's off limits to you, I don't need trouble thank you very much."

"What? Now you are my adviser?" He laughed, "the last I checked you built houses."

I was too drained to carry on a bullshit conversation, so I cut the call short and headed home.

Haile handed me a Manhattan as I sat down, just like I liked it—straight up over one big ice cube —she looked like Medusa, with her long blond curly hair cascading down her shoulders, a beauty so powerful if one looked at her too long, she could turn you to stone. Haile despite all the trauma that she had suffered as a child was strong and impenetrable who would never allow anyone to hurt her again.

"Was the weekend successful?" she asked.

"Very," I said, "everything went as planned, the feedback was great."

"Did you enjoy yourself?" she asked.

"Not really, I never do."

"Was there a particular reason?" she asked.

"Janna has become a bit of a problem; she made a play for me and honestly I don't want to get involved."

"Why not?"

"She's overbearing."

"Too aggressive?" Haile said.

"She has ulterior motives, there is something about her that I don't trust."

"Let her know that you aren't interested," she said.

"I did," I said, "she was not happy."

"Who gives a shit?" she laughed.

We barbecued steaks in the summer kitchen on the balcony that we ate with a large mixed salad, the moon was full, the waves lapping on the beach, our laughter, ringing out, what could be better than this? I thought. Home is where the heart is.

CHAPTER FOURTEEN:

HAILE

My psychiatrist urged me to confront my mother so that I could finally, as an adult, get closure. Dr. Barrow said that as long as I kept this secret I wouldn't heal. I had written all my feelings down in a letter to my mother and we burned it in a ceremony at her office. I told my doctor that even after all these years I was terrified that my mother wouldn't believe me. Dr. Barrow said that even if I was correct and she didn't believe me I still have had my say. I had always believed that it was impossible for my mother to be in the same household for all those years and not know that something was going on. Dr. Barrow agreed with me.

She said, "You are now in your forties, you are strong, and you are an adult, no matter what your mother's response is, she cannot harm you. Those days are gone, but if you don't confront her, you will be stuck in this loop forever."

I agonized about this for weeks, we went over scripts and different scenarios. I worked on my reaction to the different outcomes and how I would cope and respond to each one. We worked on retaining my relationship with my mother despite the option of negative responses. Could I even have a relationship with her if that was so? The best result would be if my mother acknowledged my pain and asked me for forgiveness that as a child, she had not protected me.

I asked Eli his opinion.

"I think you should let sleeping dogs lie," he said. "You are doing so well, why open a can of worms after all these years?"

"Dr Barrow is an authority on child sexual abuse," I said, "she maintains that I will never heal unless I confront my mother."

"You know that I will support you whatever you choose to do," Eli said. "Would you have the confrontation at the doctor's office?"

"I think that I will ask her to the condo," I said, "on home ground—I will feel better if I know that you will be there in the other room."

One sunny morning I was sitting on the patio having coffee when I spontaneously dialed my mother.

"Hi, darling," she said.

"Hi, Mom, I have something to ask you."

"Why the sad voice?" she said, "I hope no one died." She laughed.

"Could you come over? There is something important that I want to discuss with you."

"You can't tell me on the phone?"

"No. It's a very deep issue for me and I want to discuss it alone with you?"

"You are being so mysterious," she said, "I hope everything is OK."

"Can you come over this afternoon?"

"Not today, I have Mahjong," she said.

"Tomorrow morning?"

"I have bridge."

"The afternoon?"

"I have golf."

"Mom, this is serious. Please make an effort."

"Are you ill?" she said.

"Just cancel the golf and come tomorrow afternoon."

"I'll see what I can do," she said, "I have commitments; it's not that simple."

She called back to tell me that she will be at my apartment the next day at 2.00 p.m.

I never slept that night, I was dizzy and nauseous, I broke into a sweat. I had to talk very sternly to myself, "You are fine, you will be fine. It's just anxiety. I got up and took an Imitrex for my migraine."

I walked crossed the living room to Eli's suite and knocked lightly on his door.

He mumbled, "Yeah?"

"I can't sleep," I said, "I'm scared."

I went to his bed and crawled in beside him. I wrapped myself as close as I could into his back and soon, I fell asleep.

My mother was a punctual person. Reception called me at exactly 2.00 p.m. to tell me that my mother was on the way up. She was dressed for the occasion—'Crises Call.' She never left the house without looking totally done. From blown out hair, to manicured toes. Turquoise blouse, white pants, pink Chanel sunglasses, gold wedges shoes. Bright colors were her palette to stand out. I opened the door shaking but she was as calm as always flashing a bright dazzling smile even though she had to be concerned.

"Mom, sit down," I said.

"It's that bad?"

I didn't wait for any preamble I just got to the point.

"Mom, this will be hard for you to hear and it's very hard for me to tell you." She looked at me puzzled.

"I'll get straight to the point. When I was little Dad sexually abused me."

"What?" she said clutching her chest, "what do you mean?"

"When he used to take me to the back room to play chess, he would touch me and do inappropriate things."

"Why are you telling me this now? You never said this before."

"I kept it a secret for all these years because I didn't want to hurt you."

"Who else have you told?" she said.

"Just my psychiatrist, Dr. Barrow, you know that I have been in therapy for years."

"Well, don't tell anyone else, you've always had a vivid imagination. You were the apple of Dad's eye, everybody knew that. I always had to tell him not to spoil you because he favored you more than your sister and brother. I always had to tell him not to spoil you because he favored you more than you sister and brother."

"Mom, he was a pervert, he ruined my life."

"Are you sure you didn't make this up in therapy? I read that a lot of people get talked into this stuff by their therapists when it never happened."

"No Mom—this is real, this is true."

"Dad was always roughhousing with you, playing around, are you sure you didn't misinterpret this?"

"For God's sake Mother, he put his ugly, dirty penis in my mouth!"

"That's a disgusting thing to say about your father!" she said.

"He used to fuck me up my ass!"

"How dare you say that about someone who worked so hard to give you a good life that it actually killed him! How dare you use such filthy language in front of me! He was the best father anyone could have. Ask Lisa and Adam—They will tell you."

"Why would I lie about such a thing?" I said raising my voice, "Why would I make this stuff up?"

"If it's true what you're saying, which I highly doubt, then why didn't you just say No!" she yelled.

"You were there Mom, why didn't you stop this?"

"You are right, I was there, and I never ever saw or heard anything going on like you say. How dare you make up these things about your father who loved you and adored you, and all of us, until the day he died. How can you ruin his reputation?"

"You had better leave, Mother!" I said in a low dark voice, "Get the fuck out of my life, I never want to see you again."

She got up, picked up her purse, fluffed up her hair, and took out a little mirror and applied her lip gloss.

"Do you have five dollars for the valet?" she asked.

"Fuck off out of here!" I yelled throwing my cell phone at her. It hit the door and crashed to the ground.

CHAPTER FIFTEEN:

JANNA

Palm Beach was a waste of my time with regards to Eli but when one door shuts, they say another opens and voila! I met James. If I was looking for love and commitment James would not fit that mold but if I was looking for money and a good time, he fit the bill. He did not waste any time and the very next day after The Breakers weekend, we had a quick lunch and slow sex in one of his fancy hotel suites that he kept for such occasions. He had called and asked me if I wanted to meet up. I had an apartment showing but pleasure before business, I canceled and said yes.

"That was fast," he said,

"I don't play hard to get," I said.

"That's refreshing," he said.

"If we are both on the same page, then we like the same books," I said.

"Let's have lunch and then see where it goes," he said, but we both knew where it would be going.

Truthfully, I wasn't that into sex, it was the challenge of getting a man to fall for me that I was into. If he was married it was even more rewarding, the wife can put up with all his shit and I get to have the good times. James's wife looked like a lovely woman, very pretty, classy but right away she saw me as a threat, and I liked that. She with her good looks, money and the mother of his children, was afraid of me! How fragile was her marriage if her man could be lured away so fast? Why would a man risk his marriage for a romp in the bed with me? I had no problems getting a guy, my problem was, keeping him, I had to up my game.

I knew what I was getting into with James with eyes wide open. He was brutally honest from the get-go.

"I love my wife," he said, "I will never leave her or my kids."

"So?" I said, while we lay on our backs after a steamy session.

"Just want to be clear from the start," he said.

"I love my life," I said, "so I'm not going to fuck it up for you or for anyone else. The moment this isn't fun for me, I'll be out of here."

"Great," he replied, "we have an understanding."

Room service arrived with a large platter of sushi, and we asked for the table to be rolled onto the balcony overlooking the sea. James opened a bottle of Domaine Ott Rose.

"What's it like working for Eli?" he asked.

"OK," I said. "He runs hot and cold, one minute he's great and the next distant and aloof."

"He is a very sharp guy," he said, "knows his job, but I agree a little off."

"He is great to work for though," I said, "but he is hard to read."

"Is he seeing anyone?" James asked.

"Not that I'm aware of, in fact no one that I work with has ever seen him with a date."

"He has the hottest sister in town," said James.

"He does?" I said knowing full well that he did.

"Camilla pointed her out at Carpaccio in Bal Harbor having lunch with a friend. She looked like one of the models who walk around showing off outfits."

"He's an awesome boss," I said, "so that's all I care about."

"Well now you can spread some of that caring my way," he said, pulling me towards him and tousling my hair.

We came back into the room, showered, put ourselves back together and left in separate elevators. I picked up my car at the valet and headed back to the office.

"Hey," I waved to Eli as I walked past his glass office.

"Hey," he called back, "come in a second."

I turned back and walked into his office.

"I'm showing an apartment at the Four Seasons in about an hour, do you care to come with me?" he said.

"Sure," I said, "I just have a few things to see to at my desk."

"Meet me at the elevators in forty-five minutes."

The last thing I wanted to do was spend my afternoon with Eli. I had lots of work to finish, and I was still a little tipsy from my tete-a-tete. I could still smell James' cologne on my clothes, but I didn't want Eli to suspect anything. The secrets and games had officially started.

As we drove towards Surf Side, Eli was in a particularly jovial mood.

"I love when things are hopping," he said, "I feel the market is heating up."

"From your lips to God's ears," I laughed.

"I didn't know that you were religious," he said.

"I'm not," I said, "I'm more superstitious, and you?"

"I believe in a higher power," he said, "I just can't reconcile when bad things happen to good people, especially children."

"I know, me too, but they say its beyond our comprehension and if we have faith, we just accept things as they happen."

"Easier said than done," he said. "Did you enjoy the workshop weekend?"

"I did," I said, "I would have liked to have spent more time with you though."

He turned the music on louder which sent me a signal that the conversation was muted.

We stopped at the elegant entrance to the Residences at the Four Seasons Surf Club. Eli jumped out the car and opened my door before the valet could get there.

As I stepped out he said, "Great legs," admiringly.

I just threw him a coy smile as we walked into the lobby.

The apartments were stunning, each feature more beautiful than the next, if you were paying a starting price of five million dollars for your apartment, it would be expected to wow the buyer. This apartment did not disappoint. The middle age South American couple were very quiet walking through, there was no oohing and aahing. In my experience the more serious a buyer—the less they say. These people seemed used to beautiful spaces and where they may appreciate the style and design, they did not seem overly impressed. Eli and I left them to have a private discussion while we stood out on the lavish sweeping balcony looking out to the sea. We never talked about the potential buyers, that would be unprofessional.

We spoke about mundane things like how bad the traffic in Sunny Isles was getting with all the new condo construction.

"I would still prefer to live in a condo," I said, "the security is so much tighter than a house."

"Well, the LeValles house is going to be more secure than Fort Knox," he said, "but I too prefer living in my condo, I can lock the door and leave."

"The LeValles will probably have their own security staff as well," I said, "they are directly on the beach and that always is a risk."

"Camilla is paranoid about security and the kids' safety, it's actually been a bit of a nightmare working this all out."

"Is she as difficult as her husband?" I asked

"Oh God, no, James is a pain in the butt to work for, if I didn't know how to handle him, I would have walked off the job long ago," Eli said.

"He seemed pretty laidback," I said.

"You wouldn't want to cross him," Eli said, "with friends like him who needs enemies?" He laughed.

CHAPTER SIXTEEN:

ELI

I t is always a warm sunny day in Florida, but this day was extra special because the temperature had dipped, and the humidity was lower. I had promised myself a day off to lie at the pool. The weekends were my busiest time, I was usually showing condos for sale, I didn't do Open houses anymore, I left that for my sales team, my time was invested in my clients. I had just come out of the pool and was toweling myself dry, about to stretch out on the lounge chair when my phone rang, it was Jack, my mother's husband.

"Eli, your mother is in the ER," he said.

"Again? Her heart?"

"She swallowed a bottle of Unisom sleeping pills, they are giving her activated charcoal so that the drug won't absorb into her stomach," he said.

"Oh My God, is she OK? Which hospital?"

"JFK West Palm Beach—I'm not sure how she is doing," he said sounding exasperated.

"I'm on my way, it will probably take me an hour to get there," I said grabbing my clothes, taking the elevator up to my floor and jumping into my car.

My mother had done everything she could for attention for most of my life, but this was the first time that she attempted suicide. Why would she do this? She lived a good life with Jack, they traveled, had a circle of friends and she had three children. Was she so miserable that she didn't want to live anymore, and this was the ultimate drama? As I sped along I95 North to Palm Beach instead of being panicked I was angry. It seemed like my whole life was spent trying to make my mother happy. Did she really want to die, or did she want to punish her children for not being there enough for her? I had heard her say that you take care of three children and then when you are older and need help, they can't take care of one mother. Bullshit, after all I did for her, not only financially but by being there for her whenever she needed me.

When I got to the hospital I parked near the door and ran into the ER entrance, Jack was in the waiting area pacing like a caged lion. He was a man in his early eighties but looked younger, despite clothes shopping at Marshalls for bargains, he always was impeccably dressed, a light-yellow polo shirt, cream chinos and white leather loafers. His silver-gray hair was slicked back contrasting with his tanned skin.

"I was at the Hard Rock playing blackjack and when I got home, I thought your mother was asleep, but she was so still that she didn't look right, I shook her and couldn't wake her, the pill bottle was lying empty at her side, so I called 911."

An ER, a medic in pale green scrubs came over to me,

"Are you related to the patient?" he asked.

"I am her son, and this is her husband."

"She is ok for now, we have her stabilized, this is not a psychiatric facility so we will keep her overnight for observation, but I suggest you have her mentally assessed. We take a suicide attempt very seriously."

We waited until she was moved into a private room upstairs; she was not a pretty sight. She looked a hundred years old. She opened her eyes.

"What happened?" she asked, "why am I here?"

"Do you not remember why you are here?" I asked.

"Why am I not dead? I wanted to die," she whispered, "I don't want to wake up, let me sleep."

I went over and took her hand, "Mom, we can work this out, you just rest now, we can handle everything else later," I said.

"Jack, it's not your fault," she said to her husband.

"What the hell were you thinking?" he said.

She closed her eyes looking like a frail bird, she had black stains around her mouth from the charcoal that they had given her to throw up.

I told Jack to go back home and rest because she was going to sleep this off for a few hours. Shortly after he left, I felt numb, and I walked out without kissing her.

When I got home, I told Haile of the events.

"I can't say that I am surprised," she said, "she would prefer death than see you happy."

"Don't say that," I said raising my voice, "I have had enough drama for one day."

There was a voicemail from Janna telling me that the prospective buyers from the Four Seasons had made an offer, I wondered why they had not communicated to me directly.

"Why didn't they give me the offer?" I said.

"They tried calling you, but you were unavailable," she said.

"My mom was in the ER, but my phone was still on," I said.

"Well, anyway, I have it, they offered three hundred thousand dollars below the asking price."

"I don't think the Four Seasons will be interested; they are getting bids above the asking price."

"Should I send it in?" she asked.

"Wait until tomorrow," I said, "let's not act so keen."

CHAPTER SEVENTEEN

HAILE

There was something that I didn't like about Janna, I couldn't put my finger on it. From the conversations I had heard between Eli and her, it struck me that she always had an ulterior motive. She seemed to be playing her cards hoping to snare Eli into a relationship. She was the kind of woman other women distrust and don't like; she was not a woman's woman. She would pursue a man just for the game of it. She was 'that' woman hitting on the men in social situations. She would talk politics, sports, world events but always resting her hand on the man's arm or shoulder. The fact that she was gorgeous didn't help. Men looked at her with adoration that I had seen myself. The one night when Eli was away on business and I went to meet his colleagues at Morton's in North Miami Beach, after a few drinks one wife who was witnessing Janna pour on the charm to her husband blurted out in a hurtful tone, "Look how interested you are in her, if I stood on my head naked, you wouldn't even notice."

There was an awkward silence and we all carried on eating as if nothing had happened, but I did see the smirk on Janna's face.

She also said to me when we got up to leave, "Aren't you bored stiff hanging out with Eli's business partners?"

"Not at all," I said, "I wouldn't be here if I was."

"You certainly go the extra mile for your brother," she said.

"I guess I'm his eyes and ears when he is not around, because maybe he doesn't trust someone in this crowd," I said walking out to my car.

The one part of my life that I regret is the loneliness. Eli says that it's time for me let go of my past— is easier said than done.

"Don't let your father continue to ruin your life," he said, "don't give him that power over you from the grave."

I have been on anti-anxiety medication for years; I still go for therapy, and I am still isolated by my fear. If I didn't have my writing, I don't know what I would do.

Writing my novels has saved me, my writing takes me away to happier places. I self-publish and sell my books through Amazon—the sales and good reviews are enough to make me feel accomplished.

When I was a little my parents did not believe in spoiling us. We received two gifts a year, one for our birthday and one for Christmas. We would take a special drive with my mother before the holidays to the big Toys R Us store just outside our neighborhood. It stood like a giant box on a big parking lot with a mural of Jerry the Giraffe.

For my birthdays I had perused the Toys R Us catalogs that came in the mail and the year I turned twelve, Cabbage Patch dolls were all the rage. They were so popular that they sold out as soon as the shipment arrived. There were lines outside the door to get them, and parents were fighting with parents to claim one for their child. They were strange looking dolls with round squished faces, different colored woolen hair and dressed in a variety of outfits. They were cute in an ugly way. The marketing was brilliant—each doll was born in a cabbage patch and were to be adopted by the buyer—you then received an adoption certificate with the doll's name and a place to sign your name as the new parent. This made the recipient of the doll feel special. I particularly wanted a boy doll because everyone preferred the girl dolls and I felt sorry for the boys left behind on the shelves.

"Are you sure this is what you want for your birthday?" asked my mother.

"Yes," I said, "I am sure."

"Well, it is your birthday," she said with a sigh, "so you can get what you want."

I brought my Cabbage Patch doll home, his name was Charlie and I put him in his box on my bookshelf, never to be opened. Every time someone told me that I couldn't do something, I looked at Charlie and said, "Yes I can," because if he could survive from a cabbage patch to living with someone who loved him, then anything was possible.

Appearances can be misleading, I looked like a happy child. My teacher told my parents at a teacher parent conference that I was a ball of energy but with a bright and curious mind. She said that if I didn't get such good grades, she would have thought that I had attention deficit disorder. She said that it looked like I wasn't paying attention in the class, but test results proved otherwise, she also said that I was a joy to have and that I made the children laugh a lot.

"You mean like the class clown?" said my father.

"Oh no," she said, "more like a comedian."

My father liked that, he prided himself on his sense of humor. Not only was he the center of attention at social gathering with his jokes, but he could also mimic different accents and mock any speech impediment or physical disability. He had everyone laughing but at the same time feeling guilty to be laughing. I heard people say to my mother, "Your husband has the guts to say out loud what others are thinking."

My younger brother stuttered as a teenager and my father would imitate him, those were the few times where his jokes fell flat. He couldn't differentiate between being funny or mean. I only understood that much later when I knew that all three of us children suffered from low self-esteem, his mean words said in jest were etched in our brains for the rest of our lives.

CHAPTER EIGHTEEN:

JANNA

I looked up the definition of an Affair—noun: a sexual relationship between two people, one or both of whom are married to someone else. James and I are having an affair; I find it exciting. The start of an affair is always the most thrilling part—two people in a bubble enjoying themselves, cut off from the humdrum responsibilities of real life. Do I think about his wife? Not at all. Do I care? Not at all. Does he care about anyone in my life? Absolutely not. James just wants to jump into bed and hump the daylights out of me, I put up with the sex in exchange for the excitement and perks that come along with the game. We meet up at various locations—out of the way restaurants and luxury hotels to take mini staycations from our everyday lives. He gave me a beautiful Cartier gold bangle engraved with—'our commitment is no commitment, James.' He said he loved that I felt the same way about our relationship.

Like all good things that are not based in reality, living in a secluded cocoon cannot last forever, soon life starts creeping in like a fog.

In the beginning he turned off his phone, but after a few months, he started taking his calls.

"What happened to no disturbances?" I ask.

"I still have to make a living," he said.

"So do I," I said, "what exactly does a hedge fund manager do?"

"I manage pooled investment funds and get a fee and percentage of profits. Fortunately, I have been doing this a long time and they tell me that I am one of the best in the country."

"Sounds like fun," I said.

"Stressful," he said, "I have billions of dollars at risk, every day, sometimes unexpected things pop up that drive me crazy, but I love it."

James and I flew on his private jet to the Caribbean Island of St. Martin and although this was a business trip for him where he was meeting up with investors, it was a good opportunity to spend time away together. The resort is situated on the French side, close to the border of the Dutch side, with the perfect background of white sand and blue waters. The Mediterranean-style main building with patios and arches framed picture perfect water views. After we settled into our villa, we walked up the hill to Reception where the restaurant and bar were situated. Distance and cocktails are a good combination to make you forget who you really are.

"Let's go back to the room for a little nap," said James, winking.

We put the Do Not Disturb sign on the door and lay on the bed, and fell asleep, this was too good to be true.

Later that night we had dinner at the L'Oursin Restaurant. Seated on the edge of a parapet, opening out to panoramic sea views, we bantered back and forth, laughing so hard that the people around us glanced at us enviously. On the table next to us was an older couple who sat in silence hardly looking at each other. A bad relationship doesn't improve in a beautiful setting, I knew that firsthand. I once went to Venice with a man who I thought loved me, but in the most romantic place in the world I soon realized that he couldn't wait to leave. Within days Venice turned from a magical fairytale to a drab and dismal theatrical backdrop.

James had a meeting with financial investors who had flown in from surrounding Caribbean islands, I went to the swimming pool and from where I lay, I could see him on the upper deck seated with a group of men and women. I felt proud that I was with an accomplished man.

After lunch we went to the beach, holding hands like two excited children splashing in the water. The ocean was so clear that we could see little fishes nibbling at our toes. James pulled me towards him and kissed me deeply pulling my body into his.

James looked at me as if for the first time, "You are so beautiful," he said brushing my wet hair away from my eyes with his fingers.

When we came out of the water, walking towards the beach we saw that the beach attendants had set up our lounge chairs with an umbrella and an ice bucket filled with bottled water. We ordered two Pina coladas and sat in a comfortable silence, the weight of the world off our shoulders.

James's phone rang, he had fallen asleep, and I glanced at his phone lying on the small table between us— it read, Home. A voice message pinged, soon after the phone rang again. I picked it up and turned it on the silence mode so as not to wake him up.

Two hours later after we had gone up to the pool to cool off and wash off the sand, James looked at his missed messages.

The first was his ten-year-old daughter, "Daddy we can't find Mommy, pick up the phone," she said crying.

"Mr. LaValle please call me back as soon as possible," said the nanny.

Then a frantic call from his mother-in-law, "James, Camilla didn't come back from tennis, she has turned off her phone. Please call me."

"Fuck, now what?" he said to me, "she must be playing games because I went away on her birthday."

"Her birthday?" I said, "you never told me."

"It's not unusual for me to miss her birthday," he said while dialing home, "come on, we are not kids."

His brother-in-law picked up, "James where the fuck have you been? Camilla has been missing since early this morning."

"I am in St. Martin on business," he said, "my phone signal is weak, I didn't get your calls."

"She didn't pitch up for tennis this morning, Rhonda called my mom because it wasn't like her, she never misses a game," he said. "Her phone goes straight to voicemail."

"Where are the kids?" James asked.

"They are at home with my mom and the nanny, we are trying to keep them calm, telling them that she will be back soon. I called the cops a few hours ago but they said that we can't file a missing person until forty-eight hours. She could have gone somewhere. She left home in her tennis clothes and hasn't been heard of since."

James then spoke to his children. "Don't worry guys," he said, "mommy must be at a friend's house, I'll try and get a flight back home in the morning."

We went straight to the concierge to ask if he could get us a flight out of St. Martin but there were no flights to Miami until the next morning. James seemed annoyed more than anxious.

"Has she ever disappeared before?" I asked.

"She has gone missing for a few hours when she got pissed off with me, but never for this long. I don't know how she can do this to the kids, what kind of a mother would do this?"

I held my tongue because it didn't seem to occur to him that maybe something bad had happened to his wife. I was disappointed that our short getaway was about to be interrupted, but I acted as if I was concerned.

"Let's pack our things and get ready to leave in the morning," I said putting my arms around him. "You may still hear the good news that she was found before we leave."

After we had packed our, we ordered room service—we were in no mood to go out. James spent most of the evening wrapping up things with his investors, it was interesting how a week's worth of talks could be condensed into a few hours, if need be, and probably get the same results.

By the morning there was still no sign of Camilla, her family and friends had gathered at the house and were asking for help on Facebook. James and I took the earliest flight out of the Princess Juliana Airport in Saint Martin for the short flight back to Miami. When we arrived in Miami and after we cleared customs, James took a cab to his home, and I took an Uber to mine. We never kissed or said goodbye, there were more important things on his mind.

CHAPTER NINETEEN:

ELI

I was walking Marley in the dog walk at my apartment, it had started drizzling and he refused to walk further. Marley did not like getting wet, he pulled me in the direction of the door leading back to the building, while I was battling to get my fob out to swipe the lock open, the front desk spoke to me through the Intercom. Security had cameras showing who was entering or exiting the building.

"Mr. Selig, you have a young lady, Camilla LaValle requesting to come up, is that OK?"

Camilla? I was taken aback, why would she be coming over? I didn't even think that she knew where I lived.

"Sure, send her up," I said.

By the time I got up to my floor with Marley, Camilla was leaning against the wall, looking wild eyed and disheveled. She was in tennis clothes.

"Camilla, what a surprise!" I said, "What's up honey?"

She burst out crying and was shaking so badly that she couldn't get the words out, I ushered her inside, sat her down in the living room and covered her with a soft cashmere throw.

I tried to compose myself and act like this was a common occurrence.

She looked like she had been hit by a bus.

She said, "this is the end for me," between sobs.

I didn't push it and let her carry-on sobbing until she stopped.

"I told you," she said, "you didn't believe me."

"About what?"

"James, having an affair."

"He is?" I said.

"I hired a private detective and I have all the proof I need," she said in a calm clear voice. "He is in St. Martin; I have photos and everything."

"With a woman?" I said.

"Who else? A man? He isn't gay."

"What do the pictures show?" I asked.

"The two of them arriving at the La Samanna resort, all over each other. Then more photos of them practically fucking in the ocean," she said.

"Do you know who this woman is?"

She started crying all over again, tears falling down her cheeks and snot running from her nose, "Guess who the whore is?" she said.

"Someone I know?"

"Yes, you introduced them," she said looking at me in anger.

"Who?" I asked.

"That slut, Janna," she said, "I knew from the minute I saw her that she was trouble."

"Janna? Are you sure?" I asked shocked.

Camilla took out a large manilla envelope from her oversized bag, opened it and three sheets of photographs fell onto the coffee table. Clear close-up photos of James and Janna—by the pool, in the ocean, in the hotel, in bed; there was no doubt what they were up to. I was not only stunned, but I was also furious.

"Fucking, James," I said, "and that fucking bitch."

I went over to Camilla and wrapped my arms around her, and we both sat there without saying a word.

After a while she sat up and looked at me.

"Eli, I just want one favor from you. I want to stay here for a few days until I collect myself, I'm not going home."

"But everyone will be freaking out about where you are?" I said, "you can't do that to your kids and family."

"Please Eli, I'm begging you, just let me hide out here for a few days."

I determined that I could not let Camilla stay at my place, I could not harbor and abet a missing person no matter who she was, I could not allow her children and family to not know where she was.

"Camilla, you have to go and face the music back home. I will come with you but it's not right to do this to your children. It's not about James, it's about your family."

"Will you come back with me? I don't want to see his face ever again, let me just stay here a while longer."

"You are brave and strong, don't ever forget that," I said.

"I'm going to kick him out of the house, and I never want to see that cheating, bastard again."

I was not shocked that James was cheating but, I was stunned with whom, the fact that Janna was so brazen to do this after I had taken her under my wing made me realize how callous and conniving, she was. I was upset that I was instrumental in their meeting. After Camilla had somewhat calmed down, she gathered the photos, put them back in her purse, wiped the mascara off her cheeks with her fingers and we drove back to their house.

Parked outside were a bunch of cars, she told me which belonged to whom—her parents, her in-laws, her sister and her friends. When we walked through the door, there was cries of relief, everyone gathered around her.

"Thank God, you are safe," they said, "where have you been? We were worried sick."

Her two little daughters threw their arms around her wailing—"Mommy where were you? Why did you run away?"

James came dashing into the living room, "Cami, Oh My God, you are here! Are you OK? What happened?"

No one asked me what I was doing there, the focus was on Camilla. I hoped that Camilla at that moment wouldn't get into the logistics of the situation, she needed to rest and gather herself first, but that wasn't what she wanted.

She turned to James and started screaming, "You fucking asshole, don't pretend that you even care about me. You liar and you cheat, why don't you tell everyone where you have been this weekend?"

James turned white.

"What are you talking about? We've been worried sick about you, how could you just run off not telling anyone?"

"I know that you have been fucking around on your phony business trip," she said, "so don't even go there. I have proof."

"I don't know what you are talking about," he said, "you are clearly unstable."

"Get the fuck out of my house," she screamed, "I never want to see you again."

Her mother held her tight, "Cam, calm down, we can work this all out. Come to your bedroom and lie down, just rest up."

The children were crying.

James looked at me, "What are you doing here?" he asked. "Why are you sticking your nose in my business?"

I didn't answer. I told Camilla that I was leaving, and that I would call her later.

"Get into bed and go to sleep," I whispered to her, "tomorrow you can work out what you want to do, don't say anything more."

As I got out into the fresh air, I was relieved to be out of the drama, I didn't know how I got involved with all that. I thought that of all the people who Camilla could have gone to, why did she come to me?

I figured that even with her large social circle she didn't have anyone whom she trusted enough to confide in, that made me feel sad. I also wondered if there was an impending divorce what will happen to the new house? How will that impact on me? What was that idiot James thinking?

CHAPTER TWENTY:

HAILE

"**I** told you so," I said to Eli, "I knew from the minute I met Janna she was bad news."

"Don't rub it in," he said, "but you know that a million married men and women have affairs, it's not that unusual."

"She works for you, and is having an affair with one of your married clients, that's pretty dumb," she said, "are you going to fire her?"

"I don't know what I'm going to do, right now I don't want anything to do with her," he said, "I have too many other things on my mind right now. She also owes me an explanation why she sold a unit in the Four Seasons behind my back."

Marley needed to be walked, so I threw on a jumpsuit, pulled my hair into a pony, put on my over-sized Gucci sunglasses and went out to the dog walk. I wasn't in the mood for conversation but as soon as I pushed open the door, there stood my least favorite neighbor, Janet, picking up her schnauzer's poop with a plastic bag.

"Hey," she said, "can you believe that the dog walk was covered in shit?"

"It was?" I said.

"Since that Epstein family moved in there are piles of poop all over. They are not picking up after their two dogs, something has to be done."

"Are you sure its them?" I said.

"Well, we watched the security cam video, and it looks like their daughter was walking those mutts last night, they both take a dump, and you don't see her picking up."

There was a large enclosed grassed area specifically for the dogs to be walked. There were plastic bags, ties, and paper towel stations along the walkway with signs asking dog owners to pick up after their dogs. Most residents complied but there were always the few that didn't. The cleaning staff would come by in the morning to check if everything had been picked up otherwise, they did the deed.

Janet was one of the first residents to move into the building and had taken it upon herself to be the poop monitor as well as the pool guard. She took her job very seriously.

I asked her why she didn't join the condo board, and she told me that she had put her name down for consideration, but she had the lowest votes and didn't get in.

"No one wants me on the board," she said, "because then the shit will hit the fan."

She would have been an excellent detective—at night, she hid in the shadows and if anyone dared not to pick up their dog poop, she would jump out and yell, "I'm reporting you to the board and you will be fined!"

Janet Reading was a short, squat woman with blue beady eyes, she was proud to tell you that she cut her own hair, it was easy to tell, choppy and uneven. She was a lonely woman, whose husband had left her many years ago for another woman, and to add insult to injury an older woman.

"He left me for a dog," she said, "nothing to look at, skinny as a pole, wrinkled beyond, no personality and a bitch. He must have really hated me."

She took a liking to me because the first time I met her; I was sitting on a bench with my head in my hands contemplating death—this was before my anti-depressants kicked in.

As its well known, misery loves company, so she sat down beside me and told me why I shouldn't be sad because her life was so much worse. She spent the next hour telling me how much her life sucked and when she was done, I was feeling better. From that day on, it was her duty to make me realize that my life was pathetic, like hers.

On a particularly windy day, I was walking Marley when she came running up to me.

"I have the best news," she said, "we are bringing in a DNA company to take samples of the dogs' shit, test it and then match it to which dog it belongs to."

"Really?"

"We all have to have our dogs give a DNA sample, then it will be easy to detect."

"What then?"

"The perpetrator will be fined $250.00. That will teach them a lesson—maybe if we hurt them in the pocketbook they will abide by the rules."

I knew that she liked me because when Marley did his business, she grabbed a bag and scooped it up depositing it in the nearest bin.

Whenever I went down to the pool, Janet was on patrol, wearing sensible Birkenstock shoes, a safari hat with a flap to cover her neck, and a whistle around her neck.

If anyone dared to dive into the pool, throw a ball, or use rafts and blow-up toys, she blew that whistle very fast. The residents with children were annoyed with her, who was this woman telling everyone what to do? She was written up by the board for overstepping her authority, but it didn't deter her—she was on a mission.

To make matters worse her closest friend in the building was the president of the board, a woman who once ran a Fortune 500 company and now ran the building with the same proficiency—both women found a common bond through the hatred of their ex-husbands.

Janet's self-appointed job was a thankless one, she was not well liked and was called the Condo Commando behind her back.

She also didn't have any filters, she told me that she called a spade a spade and would tell you like it is, whether you liked it or not.

"As pretty as you are," she once said to me, "no guy is ever going to go for you. You and I have that same 'stay away' gene that men can smell a mile away."

Even if that was true it hurt my feelings, I didn't want to be lumped in the same category as her, an embittered old woman with a bad attitude.

"And tell your obnoxious brother to stop driving his car like a raving maniac," she said to me, "I put in a complaint to the board, so he should be getting a warning note soon."

"Oh geez, Janet," I said, "you are too much."

She shot me a look of anger, "When push comes to shove, you will all thank me for trying to protect you all. Stupid people do stupid things without thinking of the consequences."

CHAPTER TWENTY-ONE:

JANNA

We got caught—James and me—his wife hired a private detective, and the proof was in the photos. I had to give her credit for being one step ahead of the game. We were just starting out and already there was drama. Nothing in my life was going to change, I didn't give a fuck about my reputation, but James stood to lose his marriage and kids, he should have considered that before getting involved with another woman.

I didn't expect Eli to be so angry at me, you would have thought that I had cheated on him. Camilla had gone running to him as soon as shit hit the fan.

"What were you thinking?" he yelled at me over the phone, "why would you go after a married man who not only is my client but my friend? His wife is one of the nicest women that I know."

"It takes two to tango," I said, "if he was so honorable, why did he pursue me? If his marriage was that good there was no way he could have been lured away."

"You don't bite the hand that feeds you," Eli said.

"Pardon? You don't feed me, I make my own living, I work my ass off, I don't work for you Eli, I work with you."

"You certainly work for yourself," he said, "why didn't you tell me that you went and sold the Four Seasons unit from under my nose?"

"It was my deal, you didn't do anything for it, the commission belongs to me," I said.

"We share the commission Janna, this was my listing, you knew that and still went behind my back and now with this incident with James, I really think I made a mistake having you join me."

"You are such a hypocrite, Eli, you act as though you are holier than thou, but you also have skeletons in your cupboard that I can't wait to explore," I said.

"I think it is better that we part ways, Janna," he said.

"Fuck you!" I yelled, "you will be sorry to see me go."

I was livid, how dare Eli tell me how to live my life. I was a grown woman; I didn't need his or anyone else's opinion about my love life. I was even madder about the Four Seasons sale, I put in all the work, I convinced the buyers to pay full price, the six percent commission belonged to me, I deserved it.

I changed into my sneakers, left the apartment to go for a brisk walk, even though it was hot and humid, I turned into the direction of the Aventura circle on Country Club Dr. I tried to walk the three-mile trail around the Turnberry Isle Resort Golf Course once a day, it was usually busy with likeminded people and families with children but this day it was emptier than usual. I noticed a tall woman with a blond ponytail, speed walking towards me and waving,

"Janna, hey!" She called out.

Only when I got closer did I recognize a college friend of mine Kerry whom I hadn't seen since the last college reunion five years ago.

"Oh My God, Kerry what are you doing here?" I said.

"We just moved from Miami Beach to Aventura, I joined a law firm here," she said.

"How is Al and the kids?"

"He is still doing surgeries in Miami, and not too happy about the commute. The kids are doing fine, I put them in a small private school, and they like it," she said.

"What made you join a law firm here?" I asked.

"I made partner in a law firm that handle rape and sexual harassment cases and because that's my expertise I decided to join them, what about you?"

"I'm still in real estate, if you need a place to rent or buy just give me a call."

I handed her my card.

"Sure," she said, "here's mine," she added, "we must do lunch, and we will meet up, I hope soon."

"Great seeing you!" I said.

We both went on our way in opposite directions.

By the time I got back to my apartment I was feeling much calmer, there was a voicemail message from James. I first took a shower and after I had cooled down, I sat on my bed, then listened to his message.

"Janna," he said in a monotone dull voice, "I'm sure you have heard that Camilla is accusing me of allegedly having a thing with you, she has photos of us in St. Martin in compromised positions." He cleared his throat, "I do love my wife and don't want to jeopardize my marriage, I know you will understand. I'm sorry if this causes you any inconvenience and I truly wish you the best. Under the circumstances please don't contact me any longer."

"Go fuck yourself and the horse you rode in on," I said out loud, "love your wife, bullshit, that's not what you told me before, and you chased me to get into my pants scumbag!"

CHAPTER TWENTY-TWO:

ELI

James LaValle was hiding out in a suite at the Aqualina Resort on Collins Ave, while Camilla and the children stayed at their rented house. This did not look like a good omen for a marriage. James instructed me to finish building the house as planned so that they could move in and get on with our lives.

Camilla said to me, "I've contacted the top divorce attorney in Florida and am going to start proceedings."

"I don't blame you," I said, "I am just as shocked as you are."

"I told you, Eli, my husband is not trustworthy, once a shit always a shit. I have had it, I'm not going through this ever again, I am done."

I didn't know how I got involved with this drama, I guess as the saying goes, if you play with pigs, you get dirty. All I wanted was to live my life peacefully and that notion was shattered further, when a few days later, my secretary knocked lightly on my office door and with her was a burly man in a black suit.

"Mr. Eli Selig?" he asked.

"Yes," I said.

He handed me a long, white envelope, turned around and left.

I tore the envelope open, the letter was from the law offices of Jacobson, Harrington & Shapiro that stated I was being sued by Marianna Janna Cooper for sexual harassment in the workplace, it was signed by attorney Kerry Shapiro. Only then did I realize that I had been served a summons.

I had to sit down. I was lightheaded and dizzy. I never saw this coming, sexual harassment—are you kidding me? That was impossible, never did I sexually harass Janna, I tried to think of all the interactions we had and couldn't think of one time where I acted inappropriately, in fact it was the other way around, she had harassed me. I knew that Janna was going to this extreme because of spite.

She had made it clear that she was interested in me and when I didn't return her affections, she made up her mind to get nasty. I also knew that even if I was proved innocent this could be a stain on my reputation forever.

I sat in disbelief before calling my attorney Arthur Gibson and sending him a copy of the summons, he told me to come to his office immediately.

I sat across from him within an hour. I had known Arthur for a few years and had only used his services for business, this was the first time that I had a personal issue.

"Tell me how this came about," he said clearing his throat and looking at me over his reader glasses.

"I met this woman Janna Cooper about a year ago, she is a realtor with a good sales record and when she asked to join my firm, I told her that I would take her on probation," I said.

"Is that usual? "He asked.

"I wasn't sure if she would be a good fit for the company, so I gave myself an out," I said.

"Why was that?" he said.

"Although she is very successful, I felt that she may be too aggressive, I had seen her around town showing properties and I noticed that she was very pushy with her clients. That is not the way I like to do business."

"Then what happened?"

"From the get-go she started making a play for me. She would make comments on how attractive she found me and dropped hints that we should get together for dinner and such. I made it very clear from the beginning that I didn't want to mix business with pleasure."

"Did you find her attractive?" he asked.

"I didn't think of her in that way, she is a good-looking woman but all I wanted was a business relationship, I was not interested in her at all."

"Was there ever an incident?" Arthur asked.

"Well, yes, there was. After a business dinner, I had too much to drink and she came on very strong, she asked to give me a blow job and unfortunately, I gave in. It turned out a disaster, I couldn't get aroused, it became awkward and before she left, she said, 'I guess I don't turn you on.'"

"And then?"

"We both acted as if nothing had happened and carried on with business as usual."

"Was there any tension between the two of you?"

"No, not that I could tell but a few weeks later at a business conference that I had organized in Palm Beach, after the first day of workshops and a dinner, she asked me to come up to her suite in the hotel," I said.

"What did you do?"

"I made an excuse that I was tired, and I refused. She turned away from me and said, 'You are full of crap.' After that incident she was hostile at work to me."

"So, what you are telling me, this woman felt rejected by you and is now claiming you harassed her, is that correct?"

"Yes," I said.

"The document states that you made inappropriate sexual comments to her which made her feel threatened in the work environment. It also states that you one time touched her hair, and that on another occasion you rested your hands on her shoulders when looking over some files. These cases are very hard to prove because it's a 'he said, she said,' scenario. There is work to be done and this is never pleasant. I will contact her attorney and feel her out to see how serious they are to go to court," he said.

On my way home I stopped at the closest Starbucks to my home, I ordered a Venti iced nonfat latte, the barista who was familiar with me took my order, "Hey Eli!" she said, "long time, no see, have you been out of town?"

Usually, I would joke and make small talk, but now I was on guard not to be inappropriate, I was learning that being friendly could be mistaken for flirting.

When I told Haile that I was being sued by Janna for sexual harassment, she was speechless.

"I have never made any sexual references or put her in any awkward sexual situation," I said, "just the opposite this is a case of a woman feeling scorned. I didn't respond to her sexual advances, so she is punishing me."

"I can't believe this," Haile said, "you of all people, who is so mindful and respectful of everyone."

"The irony is that no one knows my secret that I can't get it up even if I wanted to," I said bitterly.

"That's a separate issue which has nothing to do with being accused of inappropriate behavior," she said,

"I am cursed with erectile dysfunction as you well know, I've been to every specialist in the entire universe, and they all concur that its psychological not physical."

"Perhaps you flirt to compensate," she said.

"I have never flirted with Janna, and now I have to spend the time, energy, and of course money to clear my name for something I didn't do," I said.

"How can a woman who is having an affair with a married man, sue another man for sexual harassment?" she said, "I don't get it."

"She is furious that she got caught and that I fired her, but the main reason was because I found inconsistencies with her finances at work," I said.

"Yes, she took full commissions for a number of sales that were meant to be shared with you."

"That's why she had to strike out at me first, to deflect her dishonesty," I said.

As soon as I walked Marley, I went to bed and I told myself there was no way I would let this woman take me down, I was too resilient for that.

CHAPTER TWENTY-THREE:

HAILE

I asked Eli for Janna's resume that was on file, I wanted to do some background checking on her that technology made easy to do. I found that she left the University of Florida in her junior year and didn't graduate there like she stated.

She was not the top salesperson at her previous Real Estate job as per her resume, and that she was married and divorced in her early twenties which she never mentioned.

I also found court records of a DUI as recent as four years ago and she was given community service hours as a first offense. This information was good ammunition to have if Eli had to go to court to defend himself—if she lied about these things she could lie about the sexual harassment.

"She sure lied about my character in her deposition statement," Eli said, "my attorney forwarded the complaints to me."

"What does it say?" I said.

"That working for me was a toxic environment, I made her feel uncomfortable with my sexist remarks, that I commented on her looks and her clothes. That I said she had great legs and that I was always trying to touch her when we were alone putting her in awkward situations."

"Was that true?" I asked.

"Absolutely not! I did once comment on her great legs, but she often told me how handsome I was, and she would touch and hug me all the time."

"You are the boss," I said, "she is a subordinate, that gets taken into account."

I went down to the mail room to pick up the mail, Janet was there.

"Why do you always dress up like you are going to ball when you are just in the building?" she asked.

"I like to dress up," I said, "does it bother you?"

"I don't give a shit, but as a good friend, I think you should tone it down," she said. "Everyone says that you are too out there," she said. "I'm just being honest. A beautiful woman like yourself doesn't need all that gunk on her face."

"Janet, please don't tell me what I should or shouldn't do, worry about yourself."

"Look at this mess," she said, pointing to the trash cans in the mail room, "everyone throws their junk mail away even when the bins are overflowing,"

"That's what they are there for," I said.

"Why can't they sort their mail up in their apartments?" she complained.

"Don't sweat the small stuff," I said.

"Do you want to grab a coffee at the bar?"

"Sure," I said.

She marched alongside, "You are so tall," she said, "it must be tough to find a man with your height."

We sat at the coffee bar overlooking the infinity pool and ordered two cappuccinos.

"Make mine decaf," she said.

The bar was bright and modern, run by two efficient young men dressed in black and white uniforms; the best perk was that the coffee and snacks were complimentary to residents and their guests.

When the waiter brought the coffee, she took a sip and said, "Are you sure it's decaf? It tastes too strong."

Enzo assured her that it was.

"When I moved here, the cups were so much bigger," she said, "they must be cutting costs."

"The sandwiches are delicious," I said.

"There used to be a bigger selection," she said, "they are cutting corners."

"I think it's great that we have this," I said.

"Do you know Kathy Greyson in 1402?" she said loudly so that the people sitting close by could hear, "I saw her stuffing handfuls of Splenda into her purse, can you believe it and she's so wealthy."

"Let her have her thrills," I laughed.

"What do you do with yourself all day?" she asked.

"Nothing," I said, "I just laze around," I said.

"I thought you were a writer," she said.

"Sometimes," I said, "when I feel up to it."

"I don't have enough hours in the day just checking up on this place," she said, "it's so badly run."

"You do a good job," I said.

"It's a thankless job, I just make enemies," she said.

"Got to run," I said, "it's time to walk Marley."

"Didn't you just walk him?" she said.

"He has a bladder infection," I said.

"Don't forget to give his DNA sample, they are doing that this weekend for the dog walk."

The good thing was that I could go straight up to our apartment in our private elevator, and I didn't have to make small talk with anyone, spending time with Janet drained me.

CHAPTER TWENTY-FOUR:

JANNA

I don't have a job, my love life is a mess, and I'm the wicked witch involved in a scandal. I will make sure that Eli will not go unpunished, he put me in this situation, and he will pay for it. When I was a young girl, I lived in fear of being ridiculed, which I always was, as an adult, after I reclaimed my power, I vowed that I would never let anyone make me feel inferior again.

In high school I was the one who never got invited to school parties, me and Debbie Carlson who was autistic. I would hear my classmates make plans for the weekend, but I was not included. If I asked to join them, they would make excuses, "We aren't going because we don't have a ride, or it's canceled because my grandmother died." When invitations were given out for birthday parties, I was left out. When I saw that everyone had an invitation in their hands but me, I'd ask to go to the bathroom, close myself in a cubicle and cry.

Valentines was the day I dreaded most. I started worrying about it from January. That was the one day of the year when anyone who had a crush could show it with a card placed on your classroom desk anonymously. Or better still by signing your name and letting someone know that you liked them. The super-markets and drug stores sold cheap boxes of preprinted little cards with matching envelopes that made it easy to hand out and slip onto a desk. Some even came with an attached lollipop. Red Carnations were also sold for a dollar by the student government to raise funds for the end of the school year party. When the fateful day arrived, I came into my class and like every other year my desk had nothing on it. My class teacher handed out candy from her, but that was meaningless to me. I never handed anything to anyone because I knew not to make a fool of myself. I told everyone that Valentine's Day was dumb and meaningless and all the others who didn't receive anything either, agreed with me.

Only after I graduated high school did I figure out why I was so unpopular. It was not only my weight and bland round face—I was the class goody two shoes, the teacher's pet. The class tattletale.

"Who erased the test quiz information on the board?" asked the teacher.

"Mark Levin and Lara McCormack," I would say.

I sucked up to all my teachers. "I love your dress Miss Chavez," I would say. "Do you need help with anything after school?"

I regularly stayed after school to clean the chalk board and tidy the class-room with the teacher and as a result most of my teachers loved me, but one, Mr. G. He actually recoiled when I approached him; he obviously abhorred class snitches and goody goodies like me. I hadn't considered that teachers were once students too and they had biases about their past classmates. I was bullied from day one in school, so I was bitter and twisted and took my revenge by getting people into trouble. I had the highest grades in my class and I flaunted them as a weapon.

"What did you get on the SATs?" I asked the most popular girl once.

"What the fuck does it have to do with you?" she said, flicking her cigarette and blowing smoke in my face in the lane behind the bathrooms.

I hotfooted to Mr. G who was on recess duty.

"Amanda Clooney, Debbie Glass and Anton Jacob are smoking behind the washrooms," I said.

"Weed?" he asked.

"Cigarettes," I said.

"Go play in the traffic," he said turning his back on me.

We went on our high school senior trip to Disney World in Orlando; it was a three-hour drive by bus. The school rented big, air-conditioned luxury buses. Fortunately, they had two toilets at the back of the bus, otherwise I would have been fixating about what would happen if I needed to pee.

Before I found out that there were toilets on board, I had told my mother that I wouldn't be going.

"What if I have to pee?" I said.

"Surely you can hold it in for three hours," she said.

"If I know that there isn't a bathroom, I will have to go," I said. Whenever my family went on a road trip, I made my parents stop every half hour to pee on the side of the highway, while my mother held a towel around me for privacy.

"You could wear a Pamper," said my mother.

"I'm not wearing a diaper!" I yelled, "what if anyone found out? Then I would have to kill myself."

My mother called the school office to inquire about bathroom breaks, and they told her that there would be toilets on board the bus, and that solved that problem.

We left at dawn and would return late that same night. While everyone was excited for the rides, I was obsessing about the food. My classmates were looking at the Disney map to see where the popular rides were located while I was looking at the eating options. Most of us had been to Disney World many times, it was close enough for a family trip for special occasions.

When we got to the park, we lined up at the entrance for security to check our backpacks for food and beverages. Disney does not allow outside food brought in, so I was told to throw away the bologna and cheese sandwiches that my mother had sent with me. The guard watched while I threw it in the garbage can to make sure that I did.

I stuck with Mrs. Jacobs, our math teacher, she was older, had a bad back and therefore walked slower. The pace of her stopping to sit on a bench in the shade because of bursitis suited me. She also had to make sure to eat snacks to keep up her blood sugar which she shared with me.

"You are going to miss the first ride because of me, Janna," she said. "You go ahead I'll be fine."

"Are you sure Mrs. Jacobs?" I asked.

"Yes, go along, you are an angel," she said, "such a caring girl."

The ride I didn't want to miss was "Its a Small World." It was too childish for everyone else, but it was pleasant and cool while we slowly trudged along in a motorized boat passing scenes of dancing dolls from all across the world. As we waited in line, we were let into the next empty boat, three at a time. I was paired with Holly and Daniel, our high school lovebirds who didn't greet me. They had been a couple since Freshman year, Holly was a cheerleader and Dan the Football star quarterback, a match made in high school heaven. They looked like the all-American couple but with a modern twist, both of them had been in and out of rehab for drug use. They were more than cool, they were frozen.

The three of us sat in the front row of the boat and they didn't acknowledge me. They looked mesmerized by the international dolls twirling around in puffy dresses, but I could see that both of them had their hands in each other's crotches, I was so entranced by the finger movements going on next to me that I forgot to watch the ride. When the boat started slowing down to let us off, I watched Daniel open a little vial, pop a pill into his mouth, then he gave one to Holly.

As soon as I got off the boat, I went straight to Mrs. Jacobs who was sitting under a tree eating a smoked turkey leg, I reported in detail what I had seen.

"Maybe it was Advil," she said, while paging our vice principal in the park.

Mrs. Jacobs told me that security found them with Oxycodone and their parents were called to come and get them.

"Thank you for being so diligent," she said to me, "I did not give your name to protect you."

"I have to pee, Mrs. Jacobs, do you know where the nearest bathroom is?"

"The closest bathrooms are out of order; I know because I just went myself. There is one way in front by the entrance."

I walked fast, then I ran because it was urgent and by the time I got to the restroom there was a long line outside the door. I felt this great sense of relief and warmth spreading between my legs, zi was horrified when I realized that I peed my pants. I took off my sweater and tied it around my waist; I looked for Mrs. Jacobs and found her eating an ice cream cone.

I whispered in her ear, "I had an accident, I peed my pants."

"Oh dear," she said, "do you want to go and see if you can buy a pair at the gift store and change?"

"I don't want to do that," I said.

"I have an idea, Holly and Daniels parents should be arriving soon to get them, do you want me to ask if they can give you a ride back home?"

That is what I did. Mrs. Jacobs arranged for me to meet them at the front office, and I went back home with them. They were in big trouble with their parents and the drive home was not pleasant. Thank goodness they didn't know that it was me who was the cause of their problems and that they were sharing a ride home with the school snitch.

CHAPTER TWENTY-FIVE:

ELI

I walked into Janna's attorney's office with my attorney Arthur Gibson, to give a deposition for the phony harassment case and I stopped dead in my tracks, sitting at an elaborate desk was my childhood neighbor, Kerry Barrett. I had heard that she was an attorney, but I wasn't aware that she practiced in Florida. Even though she was an adult, I recognized her immediately, she looked like a carbon copy of her sophisticated mother, Mrs. Barrett.

"Kerry? Kerry Barrett?" I said stunned, "the last time I saw you, you were thirteen."

She looked at me and half smiled, I couldn't tell if she was pleased or annoyed to see me after all these years.

"When Ms. Cooper called me and told me that she was suing an Eli Selig, I put two and two together and I figured it was you," she said.

"How did Janna get to you?" I asked incredulously.

"From our University of Florida days, and we have kept in contact over the years."

"You two know each other?" Arthur asked looking at us both.

"As kids," said Kerry, "we were next door neighbors in Plantation."

"This is such an awkward way to meet," I said, "I am being falsely accused of sexual harassment."

"I can't discuss this with you, its client privileges," she said, "but these are serious allegations, and we need to get to the bottom of it."

"I really think that this suit is a lot of bullshit," said my attorney Arthur, "all they really have is that Eli allegedly was flirtatious, touchy-feely tops maybe, and he admits that he once complimented her legs. If she was so uncomfortable as she alleges, then why didn't she leave? There was no contract for her to stay with his company, she was a free agent to leave at any time. There are no witnesses to collaborate her story, and Ms. Cooper never once complained to anyone, she never told a soul that she felt violated. This all came about after my client rejected her advances, and she was pissed off."

"I am not at liberty to discuss this now," she said, "Mr. Selig is purely here to give a statement for the record."

"Janna doesn't have a chance," I said, "are you aware that she is also involved in the breakup of a marriage right now?"

"The one thing has nothing to do with the other," Kerry said.

"Tell that to the wife, whose husband she is cheating with," I said.

"Eli, please keep to the issues at hand," she said.

"I think a judge will find that interesting," said Arthur.

"Come on Kerry, you knew me so well, we were childhood best friends, do you really believe that I could do this?"

"What I do know, Eli, is that you were very mean to me and bullied me so much as a child. I haven't forgotten that," she said.

"That was because I had a major crush on you," I said.

"You had a weird way of showing it," she said pursing her lips.

I left the attorney's office shaken up; I had been wrong to think that Kerry had pleasant memories of our childhood friendship.

"Lesson learned," said Arthur, "you should always be nice to everyone because you never know when something can come back years later to bite you," he scoffed.

I called my mother as soon as I was back in my office.

"Guess who I bumped into today?" I said.

"How would I know?" she said.

"Kerry Barrett, our next-door neighbor from Plantation. she's an attorney and I went to her office this morning."

"Spoiled brat Kerry?" she said, "wow, that's a blast from the past. I heard that her parents got divorced and her father lives in Costa Rica with his young wife and kids."

"They were such a close couple," I said, "what happened to Mrs. Barrett?"

"She lives off her alimony in New York, I wouldn't cry for her. What were you doing at Kerry's law office?"

"It's a long story Mom, I can't get into it now. Send my love to Jack," I said.

"He is at work, at the head office," she said.

"Work?"

"At Publix, grocery shopping, he's on a mission to find two big pieces of wild salmon for dinner tonight," she said, "he left early this morning to get the fresh catch of the day. This is serious business."

"I hope I never get to be like that," I said.

"Make sure that you have a hobby before you retire," she said, "boredom makes you do funny things."

CHAPTER TWENTY-SIX:

HAILE

Eli was very pensive and quiet. "It's strange," he said, "just when everything was going so well for me, I have to have this bullshit with Janna."

I tried to play the Devil's advocate. "Let's say this goes to court and she wins, how badly will that affect your life?"

"It affects my credibility," he said, "and who knows who else may come out of the woodwork and accuse me of crap, that's what generally happens with these things."

"Both of you are adults, she claims that you affected her mentally and she couldn't stay in that environment. There was no rape, no sexual assault, it's strictly hearsay."

"I know, how can this compare to what you went through?" he said, "your father should have gone to jail for life. Do you think that if he didn't die you would have pressed charges as an adult?"

"I often think about that, I have never had closure because he did die. He should have suffered, he needed to be punished," I said.

"I know."

"Little things affect me every day, I was having lunch with Grumpy Janet at the pool bar the other day and you know those white ceiling fans? Every time I looked at them whirring around, I started feeling panicky. My heart was beating fast, I broke into a sweat, I started feeling nauseous, I made an excuse to leave."

"This happens a lot," he said.

"You know the reason—when my father was in my room, I would look up at the ceiling fans and pretend I was flying on them to a faraway land," I said. "Now when I am in a room with ceiling fans, it takes me back to those very dark times."

"You have come a long way," Eli said, "you are strong, and you are power-ful, and he can never hurt you again."

"You are strong, and you are powerful, and this too shall pass," I told him.

The night was hot and humid but there was relief from a small breeze came off the ocean. We sat on the lounge chairs without any clothes on, there were no stars, only the moon illuminating the vast ocean and the white foam from the gentle waves rolling in. It was turtle egg laying season; the electrical lights from the streets and houses cause a disruption to the nesting process. Newly hatched turtle babies instinctively crawl towards light, and they get confused and start crawling in the wrong direction towards the artificial lighting, away from the sea. The county changes all outdoor light bulbs along the seaboard to red or amber because they are dull which helps steer the turtles in the correct direction. The hatchlings need to scramble towards the ocean and swim away for their survival. Not many survive and most are eaten by predators in the sea; but the ones who make it became a new generation of turtles. The turtle nests on the beach had been cordoned off by red tape so that no one would step over them. A volunteer group of animal right advocates help keep guard of the eggs until they hatch. On this night, we saw hundreds of baby turtles scurrying along the sand towards the ocean.

"I'm like a grown turtle," I said to Eli, "against all odds I have survived."

"Just as well you don't look like one," he laughed.

"I should act more like a turtle with a shell protecting me from bad energy and evil intentions," I said.

"I'll call you Shelby from now on," Eli said, "'shell' we go in now?"

"You are so silly," I said.

CHAPTER TWENTY-SEVEN:

JANNA

I was sitting at the Island Grill on the terrace, which is in walking distance from my apartment, having an iced coffee, it was too late for breakfast but too early for lunch. All the tennis courts alongside were filled with daily players, I could hear their grunting as they hit the balls. I had promised myself not to contact James, but then after the caffeine kicked in, I thought why not? What harm can it do? Let me take the higher road and be the mature one in the situation. I was not the jilted lover, I knew from the start what the situation was, James had made that very clear, the problem was that we got caught.

I texted him on his private cell phone, "I hope you are doing OK, and things are settling down, it's been very difficult for me too."

The message did not come back undelivered, so I knew that he hadn't blocked me, which I took as a sign that he didn't hate me.

I had heard from a common friend that he had moved out of the house and was staying at the Aqualina Resort on Sunny Isles Beach, he wanted to be close to his children. I figured that he should have thought about that before cheating on his wife. I was sure that I wasn't the first woman whom he had an affair with, but perhaps the first time he got caught.

I was married once, for three years in my early twenties to an Italian whom I met on a vacation in Italy. His good looks were what I was attracted to, but what impressed me most was that no one had ever worked so hard to win me over. He made me feel like a princess, showering me with gifts, flowers and expensive jewelry. He told me that he had never been so taken with anyone before. His accent only added to the allure, after we made love, he would exclaim, "Quanto sei bella! How beautiful you are!" No one had ever made me feel so special. He took me on beautiful drives in his red Alfa Romeo to the countryside where we picnicked in

97

sunflower fields by the river. When it was time for me to leave, he begged me to stay. He had tears in his eyes when we kissed goodbye at the airport.

"This is not goodbye," he said, "it's arrivederci, I will see you again soon."

After I got back to the States, he called me every day on the hour to tell me how much he missed me. He said that I was the one for him, and that life is unbearable without me. He wanted me to apply for a marriage visa as soon as possible. He never asked for my opinion, but I was just so grateful that a man like him wanted me.

From the minute he arrived on American soil we had ninety days to get married or the visa would be nullified. I had not mentioned him to my parents or friends because I first waited to see that he in fact would show up. I was expecting him to let me down but after he arrived, I told my parents and then immediately regretted it.

"Are you sure he isn't using you to get a green card?" asked my father.

"What do you know about him?" asked my mother. "Did you meet his family and friends?"

"Can't you just be happy for me?" I yelled. "Why do you always have to think of the worst-case scenario?" I shouted.

He settled down in my apartment quickly, and I marveled how easily he adapted to his new environment. He developed a daily routine and we fell into a pattern of domesticity. He would go for an early morning run, come back for breakfast and then work out in the condo gym. Then he would go out for a late lunch, come back home take a nap and wait for me to get home from work.

He always met me with a smile, we chatted happily about his day while I got changed and dressed to go out for dinner. He hadn't had the opportunity to change his Italian lira into dollars, so I gave him enough cash for the week. I marveled how easily he made friends and he already had a bunch of guys to play basketball with on the condo court. There was only one thing that annoyed me, he never tidied up and I always came home to a messy place with dishes in the sink, but I thought that was a small price to pay for my happiness.

Before the ninety days were up, I had arranged a small wedding ceremony and dinner at a nearby country club, inviting my parents, some cousins and a few friends. None of my family warmed to him, they were distrustful of his motives. This only alienated me from them and made me angry.

As soon as we were married, everything changed, I realized that my family were correct in their assumptions. Gone was his adoration for me and he became an absent husband. He left early in the morning and came back late at night after I was asleep. I didn't even bother to ask where he went, I think I knew. He was very popular with men and women. When I asked if he was looking for a job, he said that was what he was doing, networking.

As soon as it was legal, I divorced him. I asked me parents to do me one favor—never to say, "I told you so."

My phone pinged with an incoming text, I jolted from my thoughts. It was James.

"Please do not text me," James wrote. "I want nothing more to do with you."

"I understand," I answered.

"I promised my wife never to have any contact with you," he wrote, "I'm going to do everything I can to fix my marriage."

"That's good," I texted back, "I am at the Grill at Williams Island, I just wanted to tell you that I have your black leather jacket, so let me know if I can FedEx it to you."

I decided not to have the buffet but to order a hamburger instead, I was feeling that I needed something more substantial, soul food.

I gestured to the head waiter that I was ready to order.

"Good morning, Miss Janna," he said, "you look so pretty. What can I get you?"

"I'll have a hamburger, medium with sweet potato fries, please," I said.

"Of course. I will bring you a breadbasket," he said heading indoors to the kitchen.

As the glass doors slid open, I looked up and there was James walking towards me.

"Fancy meeting you here," he said.

I tried to talk but no words came out.

"I came to pick up my favorite jacket," he said, "I was next door at the Peninsula with a client."

I looked around the terrace to see if there was anyone that I knew; there was only a table of tennis ladies, and an old lady in a wheelchair with her caregiver.

"It's in my apartment," I said, "and I'm just about to have my lunch."

"That's fine," he said, "I will sit at the bar and have something to drink while I wait for you to finish."

I was totally thrown, I couldn't make James out, what was he thinking? By the time my hamburger came, I had lost my appetite. I took a few bites and couldn't eat anymore.

"You didn't like the food?" asked Luca when he came to remove my plate.

"I ate too much of the bread," I said.

He looked at the breadbasket that was still untouched.

"Just bring me the check please," I said.

As soon as I got up and walked inside, James left the bar to join me. We walked across the street to my building without a word.

"Do you want to wait in the lobby while I get your jacket?" I asked.

"No, I will come up with you," he said.

As soon as we got in my door, he pulled me towards him and kissed me hard.

"I have missed you," he said.

"I can't make you out," I said, "you acted like you never wanted to see me again, why this change of heart?"

"You have cast a spell over me," he said, "I can't stop thinking about you?"

"What about your marriage?" I asked.

"I'll figure it out," he said wrapping his arms around me and pulling me towards the bed.

"Stop!" I said, "I won't be your fuck buddy, I have feelings too you know?"

"That's why we can't just end this like nothing ever happened," he said.

I picked up his jacket from the chair and threw it at him, I opened the front door, "Get out," I said.

As he left, I couldn't make out his expression; it wasn't hurt, more bewildered and disbelief that I would have the nerve to kick him out.

I was proud that I had the courage to stand up to him, I stood with my head against the door for a long time before I realized that I was weeping.

CHAPTER TWENTY-EIGHT:

ELI

My mother, who is nosey, wanted to know why I was seeing attorneys, so she came over to my office. She only came to the office if she had to find out information immediately. She knew that I wouldn't be short with her in front of my colleagues. I never felt comfortable talking about personal matters in hearing distance from my staff, so I took her down to the lobby cafe.

My mother always dressed correctly for the occasion—she had a collection of outfits for different themes—dinner parties, lunch dates, the theater, casual walks, doctor's appointments, funerals and personal crises. She came dressed to see me in the latter. She wore a navy pantsuit with a crisp white blouse and flat Ferragamo shoes. A red and navy scarf tied loosely around her neck gave her the air of an aged flight attendant. Her thick bleached blond hair was tied back in a low ponytail and with oversized tortoiseshell sunglasses she looked the picture of Confidential Concern. My mother had come a long way from her TJ Maxx outfits, now that she was married to Jack she could afford to shop at upscale stores.

"So, tell me why you had to see Kerry as your attorney?" she asked taking a sip from a cappuccino with a slight tremor in her hand.

"Kerry isn't my attorney, she is representing a disgruntled ex-employee of mine who is suing me for something that I did not do," I explained trying to keep my voice down.

"Such as?" she asked.

"Sexual harassment, which is totally unfounded and untrue," I said.

"What do you mean?" she said with her bottom lip quivering in the same way it would when I had done something bad as a child.

"It's just her way of getting back at me," I said, "revenge for not falling for her romantic interest in me. I also let her go for being disloyal and dishonest."

"Did you ever do anything sexual to her?" said my mother looking me straight in the eyes.

"No, Mom, please, I would never do anything like that, you know me."

"Why then would she want to take this to court if she didn't have any evidence?"

"Because she is screwed up and trying to get back at me and make some money," I said raising my voice.

"Do you have a good attorney?" she asked.

"Yes."

"Why would a smart woman like Kerry Barrett represent a person who doesn't have a case?"

"Do you think that I could ever sexually harass a woman?" I asked.

"I don't know Eli," she said, "you are a bit of a dark horse."

"What does that mean?" I asked.

"I have always been concerned about you; your personal relationships have been quite weird. You are in your forties and never have had a committed relationship, you are very secretive about your dating life. I have some reservations about you," she said, "most of your friends are married with children and you are just..."

"Wait a minute, mother, are you suggesting that I could be guilty of this?"

"I just don't know Eli, something doesn't add up," she said, "I'm not the only one who thinks this."

"Who the fuck are you discussing my private life with?" I said.

"Jack, your sister, your brother, we are all concerned about you."

"I can't believe this," I said, "I'm an adult, I wouldn't discuss who I am dating or not dating with my mother. I am beyond shocked and hurt that you would even intimate that I may be guilty of this phony lawsuit. You know me better than most."

"I don't really know you anymore Eli, you have rarely been there for me when I needed you, if it wasn't for Jack, Lisa and Adam I don't know where I would be. I haven't been well for ages, and do you ever call to ask me how I am?"

"I've had enough of this," I said, "I have always been there for you Mother, it's just the opposite, you have always been too self-involved to have ever been there for me. So, let's just end this charade here and now."

I got up, paid the bill and handed her ten dollars for the valet.

"If you see Kerry again, send her my best," she said, "she was such a lovely girl, I had always dreamed that both of you would get together.

When I got back to my office, I realized that I was trembling, I couldn't believe what had just happened. If my own mother had doubts about me then why would a judge believe me? The more I thought about it the angrier I got and the more I wanted to prove my innocence. The only complaint that Janna had was that I may have been flirtatious or maybe touched her in a non-sexual way. The tryst in Palm Beach was two consenting adults engaging in a sexual act and that was not a crime.

CHAPTER TWENTY-NINE

HAILE

Marley didn't look well, he was lying on the living room floor, trembling and panting.

"What's wrong, baby?" I said.

Marley lay barely moving with a small amount of white foam on his lips. I started to panic and knew that I had to get him to the vet as fast as I could. I scooped him up in a blanket and rushed out to my car. I lay him down in the back seat and pressed the elevator button on my dashboard to take us down. Every traffic light was red and when I finally pulled up to the veterinary hospital, I raced out with him in my arms.

The clinic staff seated in the front when I walked in, took one look at Marley and ushered us into an examination room.

The vet, Dr. Nguyen was fortunately on duty, and she knew Marley well as a patient.

"What is going on?" she said.

"He was perfectly fine until this morning, I found him lying, breathing heavily on floor," I said.

She examined Marley and within minutes told me that unfortunately he had what they call Bloat.

"What is that?" I asked.

"The stomach fills with air, pressure builds, stopping blood from returning to the heart. Marley's stomach has flipped, and we have to take her in for an emergency surgery," she said, calling for her assistant.

"How did that happen?" I said shocked.

"It happens usually to larger breeds when they eat too much too fast, but it can happen for various reasons," she said.

"Will he be, OK?"

"We are going to do everything that we can, but I can't guarantee that," she said, "this is very serious."

I patted him and whispered, "You are going to be fine, I promise," I said.

One of the staff gave me a pile of forms to fill in and sign, as soon as I was done, they whisked Marley away.

Dr. Nguyen looked back and said that I should call Eli.

"He is out of town," I said, "he will be back soon."

I sat in the waiting room in a daze, a young teenage boy with an Australian sheep dog tried to engage with me but I was in another zone.

"My dog has a cough," he said, "my parents told me that if I get a dog, I am responsible for any vet fees, would you know how much this visit will cost?"

"Ask the front desk," I said.

"I did and they said that they can't give me a number until the vet has seen my dog. I hope that I have enough money," running his hand through his hair nervously.

"Well, my dog may die soon and I'm a wreck but please don't worry about the money," I said, "just tell them that I will pay, they can put it on my card on file."

"Wow, I can't do that, are you sure? Can I like clean your car or something?"

"Just shut up and take the money," I said.

Marley meant the world to me, I loved him dearly, I couldn't bear to think of him suffering. He had looked at me with such sad, confused eyes when the vet carried him away. I had to stop myself from running into the surgery to see how he was doing. I kept asking for an update.

"Miss Giles," the girl at the front desk said, "why don't you go home, and we will call you when he is in recovery?"

"I will rather wait here," I said, "please put this kid's costs today on my credit card."

"Thank you so much," the boy said, "you are a kind lady and I hope your dog is OK."

When Dr. Nguyen came out, I could tell by her expression that something was wrong, my chest tightened.

"How is Marley?" I asked, "can I see him?"

She looked at me with sad eyes and said, "I'm so sorry, we did everything that we could, but Marley didn't make it."

"What do you mean that he didn't make it?" I asked.

"Marley, passed away, I'm sorry, there was nothing we could do to save him."

"He died? You couldn't unbloat him?"

"It was too late, I'm sorry."

I dropped to the bench stunned.

"My friend has some puppies, I can get you one," said the boy.

"Shut up!" I said.

Someone led me into a private room that had shutters on windows and glass doors, that must have been the Grieving room.

"It may help you to know that Marley felt no pain, he just fell into a peaceful sleep," one of the staff said.

They left me in the room to give me privacy to process the loss, it had happened so fast. I felt a deep sense of grief, but I did not shed a tear. I would have given anything to cry just to get some relief from the pain, but no tears came.

I just felt empty and numb.

An assistant came in to check on me.

"How will we bury him?" I asked.

"We do cremations and then we will give you the ashes," she said.

She showed me a catalog with the different choice of urns.

"I'm sorry," I said, "I can't do this now, please take that away."

"I understand," she said, "we can talk about it some other time, but we don't have the space to keep Marley in the fridge for too long."

As I walked out, the lady at the desk said, "We processed your credit card, do you want to see the final amount?"

"No," I said.

When I got home, I collapsed into Eli's arms.

"Marley is dead," I said.

"I know you texted me," he said.

"She died of the bloat."

"It's so sad," he said.

"I am heartbroken," I said.

"Me too, I loved him."

We sat on the sofa in shocked silence staring at Marley's empty dog bed and chewy toys until the morning light appeared.

CHAPTER THIRTY:

JANNA

left my apartment for my evening run, I always have hope that when day turns to dusk, just before the sun sets, the weather will cool down. This was not to be and as I began to pick up pace my hair was already damp and my body breaking into a sweat. I had lived in Florida all my life, but I still couldn't adjust to the heat. I run daily from Williams Island to the Aventura circle and jog the four miles from one end to the other. There are always runners, walkers, and cyclists from dawn until late at night. I like to run in silence without music or interruption and use this time to look at nature around me, the trees, the green grass of the golf course, the changing sky, the singing birds, I try not to let intrusive thoughts of despair engulf me. I pass people whom I know but I don't acknowledge them. On the way back at the point where I started there is a Starbucks at the entrance to the Turnberry Resort, I stop and order a large iced green tea and sat down at an outside table to take a small break before I head home. I hear someone calling out to me.

"Bitch," she says.

I look up, its Camilla LaValle.

"Are you talking to me?" I ask.

"Leave my husband alone and fuck off," she said loudly, "or you will be sorry."

"Excuse me?" I said, "I have nothing to do with your husband nor do I want to."

She was wearing a golf shirt with a gray skort, hair pushed under white cap and even with her sunglasses I saw pure hatred in her face.

"He hates you," she said, "so stop trying to mess with him."

"FYI," I said, "I dumped him, but he keeps trying to get me back."

She picked up my plastic cup of iced tea and threw it at me, hitting the side of my forehead; the lid flew off and the tea with ice, rolled down my face. Everyone sitting at the outdoor tables gasped.

"What the fuck?" I yelled.

"That will teach you to stay away from my husband," she said stomping off towards her car.

Someone said, "call 911."

I said, "Please don't she's just a psycho."

An elderly woman sitting alone with her yorkie terrier by her feet called out to me, "You shouldn't mess around with married men."

"And you should mind your own business," I answered wiping myself down with napkins.

I walked the rest of the way home, went upstairs to change my clothes and called James.

He picked up after one ring. "Guess what just happened?" I said, "your wacko wife followed me to Starbucks at Turnberry, accosted me and threw my iced tea in my face."

"What?" he said.

"You had better warn her to never to do that again, or I will have her arrested for assault."

"I bet you will," he laughed, "I heard about you suing Eli."

"It's not funny," I said, "I'm not going to tolerate public humiliation from that nutjob."

"Calm down," he said, "come on over and we will discuss this, I am at the Aqualina, suite 908."

"You promise you won't touch me?" I said.

"Scouts honor," he said, "come over for a drink, I'll get you another iced tea."

I called for my car, hopped in and drove down 163rd Str, over the bridge to the Aqualina resort. My car was the only one that wasn't a Rolls Royce that pulled up to the valet.

"Welcome back," said the doorman, who recognized me as a regular at the Il Molino Italian restaurant there.

I tapped on the door, James opened it looking very sallow and tired, he was wearing a spa terry cloth robe.

"Good to see a familiar face," he said.

"You look a mess," I said.

"Divorce is not for the faint of heart," he said.

"What happened to the reconciliation?"

"It's just such a long story, come on in, can I get you something strong to drink?"

"A glass of white wine would be good," I said, "I'm still shaking over that unpleasant incident."

I sat down on the soft pillowed sofa, took a sip of my wine, kicked off my shoes and immediately felt better, part of that was because I was sticking it to Camilla, I wouldn't let her dictate to me whether I can see her estranged husband or not.

"What made you have a change of heart to see me?" he asked.

"It's my prerogative," I said, "after your wife threw ice in my face, I realized that she already views me as a villain so I might as well play the part."

He sat down next to me on the sofa and took a sip of his scotch and soda, "The thing that sucks the most is that I miss my children so much."

"Then why aren't you trying to fix things with Camilla?"

"The truth is, I have never been happy with Camilla, we are very different people, we are like two ships passing in the night. The only thing that keeps us together are the children, but that's not enough for me."

He cupped my chin in his hands and leaned in to kiss me.

"You promised that you wouldn't," I said.

"I said, scouts honor, but I am not a scout," he said, "so it doesn't apply."

"You are such a bastard," I laughed, "that's why I love you."

"You said the 'L' word," he said, "I think I'm going to faint."

"Not that kind of love," I said, "like I love your car, kind of love," I stammered.

The best thing that we had in common was that after sex, we both pre-ferred to sleep alone, in separate beds, there was a second bedroom, so I went in there and slept better than I had in months.

CHAPTER THIRTY-ONE:

ELI

C amilla called screaming, "That fucking whore got in my face and accosted me at Starbucks."

I was driving and almost swerved off the road, "Who do you mean?" I said,

"Who else? That fucking Janna," she yelled.

"Where are you?" I said.

"At home, where do you think I am? About to slit my wrists," she said.

"I'm coming right over," I said.

I turned my car around and drove to the rental home where Camilla and her kids were staying while the new house was being built. James had been kicked out and was holed up at the Aqualina Resort and Spa.

I rang the doorbell and immediately the dogs started yapping.

"Stop Vinnie!" Camilla yelled to her dog.

Camilla opened the door and at first, I almost mistook her for the house-keeper. She had shrunken in height, she had expanded in girth, her abundant golden hair was now greasy and stringly, her eyes were sunken, and her pallor was gray.

"Cami?" I said just to make sure.

"I'm her ugly twin," she said, "who the fuck do you think it is?"

The house was a mess, toys all over the place, wilted flowers in the vases, where was the cleaning staff?

She read my mind.

"I instructed the staff just to take care of the kids, I don't want them around in my space vacuuming, I need peace and quiet," she said.

"What happened at Starbucks?" I asked.

"I saw the bitch going into Starbucks, I had just finished my round of golf at Turnberry, so I followed her in and read her the riot act," she said, "she's not going to go flaunting herself around town after ruining my marriage."

"And then?"

"She had an attitude with me, who does she think that she is? I picked up her drink and threw it at her."

"That's it?" I asked.

"She got what she deserved," I said.

She called out to her housekeeper, "Gracie please make a salad, and some veggie burgers."

"I can't stop eating from nerves," she said. "You know, I tried so hard to be the perfect wife, I tried so hard to keep James happy, but in the end, it meant nothing. I killed myself to always look young and sexy, but he always had a roving eye, I was never enough. Yesterday, I saw him at the office of my attorney who is handling the divorce. He said to me, 'Geez, you've let yourself go.'"

"You have been a wonderful wife and mother," I said to her, "and the best-looking woman around. He will regret losing you, for sure."

"Look how fat I've got?" she said.

"Oh please, you are still a hottie," I said.

"Look at you," she said, "not a wrinkle, not an ounce of fat, always perfect. It's so much easier being a man."

"That's not true," I said, "I struggle with my emotions, self-image, trying to be perfect both in my social and professional life, it takes its toll. Are you aware of what I'm going through with Janna?"

"What can the slut do worse to you than she has to me?" she said.

"She is suing me for sexual harassment in the workplace."

"Are you kidding me?"

"I wish I was. She is accusing me of inappropriate behavior towards her."

"That is absurd, she is a sexual predator, she chased James from the minute she met him, she's after the money, that's all its about."

"So, we are both going through shit from the same person," I said. "I wish I had never met her."

The housekeeper brought in a tray and put it on the coffee table, Camilla's chihuahua immediately jumped up and started sniffing and licking the food.

"Vinnie, get down," she said, pushing him off. "Don't mind him, he is clean, just came back from the groomer." She lifted him up and kissed him on the mouth to prove a point.

The three children were at summer camp.

"They are really messed up about our split. Sasha who is eleven is struggling with this the most, she hates her father for doing this to us. The other two don't show their emotions but are acting out in different ways—with anger and violence. All three are going to therapy. The therapist told me and James not to talk badly about each other in front of the children, but that's not easy. They hear me calling him an asshole and worse, and he tells them that their mother is a selfish bitch who never loved him."

"Do you think that you would ever take him back?" I asked.

"I hate him so much that I will never take him back, but anyway, he doesn't want me, so there isn't any point in what I want."

"Have you both tried marriage counseling?"

"I once asked him to go with me and he said over his dead body."

I looked at Camilla eating her burger with sauce dripping down her chin, she looked so sad and vulnerable. I had always known her as this spunky, perky, confident woman and I felt that sometimes life can be cruel. We are complicated beings; we all want love and to be loved and unfortunately, we just keep messing up.

CHAPTER THIRTY-TWO:

HAILE

After Marley died, I didn't allow myself to feel sad and depressed, I pushed the darkness away and told myself to get over it. I had trained myself to do this efficiently since my childhood traumas with my father.

Janet said, "Go and get yourself a puppy immediately, so that you can replace Marley and feel better."

"I don't want to replace Marley," I said annoyed, "no new dog will replace him, he was not disposable."

"A new dog will distract you," she said, "I've known women who have lost a baby and immediately conceive another."

"That's crap," I said, "you can never replace anyone in your heart, you never get over it."

"Well, my husband replaced me very fast, so obviously one can," she said.

I was going to say that it's obvious that her husband didn't love her, but I kept my mouth shut.

She had once told me that her ex-husband was a very frugal man despite being wealthy. He complained when she bought designer clothes, shoes or handbags.

"You don't have to shop at the most expensive stores," he said, "Marshalls has all the labels for less."

He gave her his late grandmother's diamond ring when they got engaged and then never bought her a gift again unless it benefited him too, like a Dyson vacuum cleaner.

He did like to eat at fancy restaurants and go on expensive cruises.

"He had to take me with him, he couldn't go alone," she laughed bitterly.

"The thing that killed me the most," she said, "was when I saw his wrinkled lizard 'ho' of a wife, wearing a huge emerald cut diamond ring. She only dresses in top-of-the-line designer clothes and drives the biggest Mercedes. What does she have that I don't?"

"Maybe it's the sex?" I said. "Look how Prince Charles of Britain preferred his mistress Camilla, who looked like a horse compared to his younger more beautiful, sexy wife, Diana."

"Yup, this dried out prune does have a big mouth, maybe it's good for something," she said.

Matters of the heart are very complex, it's hard to define what attracts one person to the other. Most of my writing is focused on that dilemma. Since the beginning of history lust has been the downfall of some of the greatest leaders. I am just pleased that I don't have that problem. I wonder how I would have lived my life if I was normal.

"Haile, why do you never date?" asked Janet squinting her eyes intensely at me.

"How do you know that I don't" I said.

"I've known you for five years and never seen you with a man," she said.

"Maybe I prefer women," I said.

"I haven't seen you with a woman either," she said.

"Well, Janet, why have I never seen you with a man or a woman either?" I asked.

"I guess you are right," she said, "but you are younger, prettier and thinner than me."

"I don't really broadcast my personal life," I said surprised that she had actually complimented me.

"Let me give you some advice," she said, "you are very standoffish, people have said to me, 'what's up her ass?' You give the impression of being stuck up and aloof, try to be more friendly."

"I'm just shy," I said.

"I know that," she said, "but no one else would, and you always dress like you want to hide from the world, covered up with long hippy dresses, hats, sunglasses, like Greta Garbo reincarnated."

"You can be very mean," I said, "you really are insulting."

"I'm just telling it like it is, that's me, honest to a fault," she said, "I'm only trying to help you."

"I don't need your help, Janet, you are not the best people-person to be criticizing others," I said.

"You are so sensitive," she said, "that's another problem you should work on."

I walked away feeling deflated, how could I let an old bitch make me feel so bad about myself? As soon as I got upstairs, I opened a bottle of wine sat at my computer and tried to write. I looked at Marley's empty dog bed which I couldn't put away yet and started crying. My sniffs, turned into sobs and the sobs into a full wailing, it was like a deep tsunami opened up and forced its way out of my mouth. I was gasping with intermittent silences as I tried to catch my breath. I was crying for Marley, I was crying for my inner child that was destroyed, I was crying for the empty shell that I had become, I was crying for not knowing who I was and where I fit in. Then it stopped, just like that. I blew my nose, wiped my tears, held onto Marley's blanket and fell into a deep sleep on the carpeted floor.

CHAPTER THIRTY-THREE

JANNA

My attorney Kerry told me that I shouldn't join another real estate agency right now. I was planning on moving over to Sotheby's, but she explained that it would make my case stronger if I proved that I was too emotionally distraught to work. When my agenda is clear and I have no impending commitments, I travel—that is my escape from reality. I put my kitty in boarding and boarded a flight to Provence, France.

From Marseille, I put down the roof of my rented Mercedes convertible and drove the familiar road to Saint Remy de Provence where my dearest friends, Jacques and Henri owned, and ran, a hotel which they had remodeled from an ancient farmhouse.

It was not a fancy place, but a clean and cozy one. My regular room, the St. Remy was available and when I arrived and unpacked, it felt like I had come home. Nothing had changed from year ago, even the tray with an electric kettle, the jar of instant Nescafe, the cups and sugar was exactly like they were the time before. The same dark wood furniture placed in the same position, even the pillows were identical, three soft, one hard and lumpy. The only change was that I had requested a mirror above the desk so that I could fix my hair and make-up. The first thing I did was open the glass doors, go out onto the balcony and check if the tallest Cypress tree I had ever seen, had grown—it had. It was impossibly high, and you could barely see the tip that reached into the sky. The manicured landscape was dotted with clusters of flowers, lavender, an array of ornate water fountains with large stone sculptures dotted in between. The suite was on the first floor with its own entrance and steps leading up to the door.

Jacques arrived, climbing two steps at a time, "Hello cheri," he said kissing me on each check and then another kiss for good luck. He was a handsome man, dressed European style with tight blue pants, body fitting shirt and red Chelsea boots. I didn't speak French, so it was a bonus that he spoke fluent English.

"So happy to see you," he said, "I hope all is well?"

"Yes," I said, "everything great, I just needed to get away for a while."

"Settle in and we will see you for dinner tonight," he said.

Whenever I stayed at Les Mas des Carassins I ate most of my meals there. Jacques and Henri engaged an excellent chef whose delectable gourmet cooking had a reputation amongst locals and visitors as 'the' place to eat in Saint Remy. In the summer months dinner was served outdoors under the olive trees and even though this visit I was alone, I sat at my regular table.

The first time I came to stay at this hotel was on a trip with an older man, a widower, whom I dated in my thirties. He was building a house in the area and was staying at the Mas until its completion. Our relationship didn't last but my love for Provence did.

It was warm outdoors but there was a faint breeze as I sat down to dinner. The evening sky was so clear that the stars appeared unblinking like animals' eyes caught in a headlight.

Henri walked towards me with a big grin, "I knew you would be back; a year is too long for you to stay away."

He did not kiss me hello as he would have if we were alone but being the ultimate professional, neither he nor Jacques made any of their guests feel less special. Over the years I had learned that they would not give anyone preferential treatment. They treated everyone equally and if we were going to talk about personal things it would be when we were in private.

He brought over, a bottle of sparkling Badoit water and my favorite bottle of white wine from a neighboring winery in St. Remy. Soon after I received the trio starter of the night—duck presented in three different ways, in small white dishes.

"You start from the left to the right," he said.

The chef was very particular with the blending of flavors as each bite was specifically choreographed. Most of the diners were couples of mixed backgrounds. A lot of the guests were regulars who booked the same week every year to be there. This visit I was out of sync with my usual timing where I had come to know the repeat clientele, most from Paris, Europe and America.

I noticed a woman also seated alone to my left; I had never seen her before. While I was used to dining by myself, she seemed uncomfortable. She kept glancing at her phone placed on the table where she could reach it easily. I got the impression that she was using it as a crutch to hide her shyness. I tried to engage and smiled at her, but she quickly looked away. She was older than me, her grey spiked short hair and pointed facial features resembled a Crested Cockatoo with big eyes. By the time our cheese platters arrived and a glass or two of wine was imbibed, she glanced over at me.

"Hello," I said, "do you speak English?"

"Yes," she said, "I am American."

"So, am I," I said, "which part?"

"San Francisco, and you?

"Miami," I said, "is this your first time here?"

"Yes, and yours?"

"I have been here a few times over the years," I said.

"I was supposed to come with a girlfriend but at the last moment she got sick, so I decided to come on my own," she said.

"There is so much to see and do in the area, even if you just stay in Saint Remy, you will have a great time."

The next morning, I bumped into her at the breakfast buffet, I asked if she would like to join me at my table. On my tray was an assortment of pastries, croissants, baguettes, cheeses and scrambled eggs with truffles. She had a banana and some grapes.

We sat down at a table by the window overlooking the beautiful gardens.

"I'm not a breakfast person," she said, "but I'm going on a tour of the nearby towns in a small van this morning, so I figure that I should have something to eat."

"Good idea," I said, "ones?"

"Gordes, Le Baux and Avignon," she said.

"You will love them all," I said. "I am going to lie out at the pool today and later take a walk into town. By the way I'm Janna, what is your name?"

"Selena," she said.

I sat under an umbrella in the heat of the day, I took a dip in the pool to cool off. There were other people at the pool, some reading, some sleeping, and it was silent except for the loud clicking of the cicadas. Instead of feeling at peace I was restless. James texted and at first, I wasn't going to even open the text, but my curiosity got the better of me and I did.

"Can you believe that the bitch changed the locks on the house?" he wrote, "my name is still on the lease, it's not legal."

I quickly put an automatic message on my phone that I was out of town. Let him wonder. I left the pool, went back to my room, showered and changed then took a walk down the hill into town.

When I got to the main road, I crossed over and walked through the arch into the maze of narrow cobbled streets to the little central piazza. I sat down at the cafe and ordered a coffee and a salad.

"Janna!"

I turned around, and there was Selena waving from across the square.

She walked towards me, "I asked the tour driver to let me off in town, I'm exhausted, can I join you?" she asked.

"Of course, have a seat," I said, "would you like something to drink?"

"Water would be great," she said, "I had a great time but quite honestly the heat nearly killed me."

"Coming from Florida, I'm used to it," I said, "but the air conditioning here isn't as efficient."

"It takes guts to travel alone," she said, "I'm finding this a little tough. It's so much better sharing things with someone. I really wasn't sure if I could handle coming solo on this trip."

"Good for you for making the effort. It's tough to be out of your comfort zone," I said.

"I hope you don't mind me asking but what brings you here on your own?"

I took a sip of my coffee. "I am at a crossroad in my life," I said, "long story short, I had an affair—a married man, we got caught and all hell broke loose."

"Matters of the heart are just the worst," she said, "I'm actually here not because my girlfriend was sick, but because she broke up with me. We were a couple for five years."

"I'm sorry," I said, "it does help to run away from one's problems. To add fuel to the fire, I am in the midst of a court case—I'm suing my ex-colleague for sexual harassment. That is also taking a toll on me."

"That sucks," she said, "how is that going?"

"In reality he doesn't have a chance but logistically it's my word against his, and you know how that goes? Men have the upper hand."

"Did he force himself onto you?" she asked.

"It was a daily thing—comments, gestures, touching."

"Oh man, that is rough, are you taking him to court?" she asked.

"I just want him to pay for what he did. If it's not jail time, then monetary. He needs to learn a lesson."

"I agree," she said, "too many victims stay quiet because they are afraid that they won't be believed, I feel for you. Keep strong."

I paid the waiter, and we left the table together to walk the uphill climb back to the hotel, I really liked this woman—she had an open and kind nature that I missed from the people in my life.

CHAPTER THIRTY-FOUR:

ELI

I closed my office door and called Kerry Barrett, Janna's attorney.

"Hi Kerry, its Eli, how are you?"

"Fine, why are you calling me?

"You and I are childhood friends, we know each other pretty well, right? I just want to appeal to your common sense, why would a person like me be in a sexual harassment case?"

"Eli, it is not OK for you to call me, I am representing your accuser and my loyalty lies with her one hundred percent," she said.

"Your parents treated me like one of their own," I said to her, "you were like a sibling to me, how can you believe the bullshit that is being thrown at me?"

"Eli, very good people do stupid things. Look how my father left my mother for another woman, who would have ever thought that?"

"I know, I heard about it, I honestly couldn't believe it. Janna Cooper is breaking up a lovely family just as we speak, and at the same time suing me for sexual harassment, does that make any sense to you?"

"Eli, I don't want to discuss this any further. Please don't call me directly again, if you want to say something have your attorney call me," she said ending the call.

I wasn't surprised that she couldn't talk to me, but I wanted to plant a seed of doubt in her mind. I was not going to let Janna Cooper tear me down. I would use every tool I had to squelch this asinine situation.

Then, I called James LaValle.

"Hey," I said, "have you been to the new house lately?"

"Of course," he said.

"We are doing the interior finishes soon; the designers will be coming next week. Who is going to give them input, you or your wife?"

"Camilla," he said, "why wouldn't she?"

"I am just checking up under the current circumstances," I said.

"The house is continuing as planned," he said, "I fully intend for us to live there as a family; me, Camilla and the kids."

"That's all I need to know," I said.

Next, I called Camilla.

"Hey, Cam-Cam, do you have time to meet me at Starbucks across from you for a quick coffee?"

"Give me ten minutes, I'm still in bed," she said, "I cancelled tennis today, I'm not up to it."

I arrived at Starbucks ordered two Grande lattes with Almond milk, a lemon loaf and a cinnamon coffee cake, I took them to an empty table and waited for Camilla.

She arrived with her Chihuahua Vinnie, poking his face out of her Louis Vuitton bag. I got up to greet her and he growled and nipped my cheek, as I leaned in.

"Jesus, what a monster!" I said.

"He is very protective," she said, "he is my bodyguard, and now I need him more than ever."

Camilla's eyes were swollen, she looked like she had been crying for days.

"I want to run some things by you about the house. We are ready for the interior designers to come in and do their thing. Do you want to confer with them for what you would like?"

"Of course, I do, why wouldn't I?" she asked.

"What are your intentions at this moment of the status quo of your marriage? The reason I'm asking is that if there should be a divorce the house would become an asset to be divided between you and James."

"My intentions are to get a divorce. I have thought about it, and I'm done with him. I can't live my life insecure always fearing that he is looking for another woman. He is begging me to reconcile but I don't want to. Even my children's nanny told me that he hit on her recently."

"What about the new house then?"

"We will finish it as planned, I will see to it that I have everything that I want built there, the house will be mine. Me and the kids will move in and live there after the divorce," she said.

"Sounds like a good plan," I said, "make sure your attorney gets that signed and sealed."

"Eli," she said taking a sip of her coffee, "why have you never married?"

"Marriage is something that I just knew from quite young wasn't for me. I'm a complicated person, Cam, I just can't see myself being with a woman twenty-four seven for the rest of my life."

"Were you ever in love?" she asked looking at me intently.

"No, never."

"That's kind of messed up," she said, "I have loved a few people in my life and its ironical that I chose the wrong one for me. I loved James dearly, but not anymore."

Camilla was the kind of person who puts on a tough façade, but I could see right through it. She was sensitive, almost fragile and her clear blue eyes revealed a deep sorrow.

When I came home, the last call of the day was to Clint Yarrow, the Private Investigator I had engaged to find out background information about Janna Cooper.

"Clint," I said, "any updates?"

"She has gone to Europe but I'm not sure yet exactly where she is situated, I'm working on it, I'll keep you informed," he said.

"Thank you," I said.

CHAPTER THIRTY-FIVE:

HAILE

"**A**ny thoughts about your fiftieth birthday party?" I asked Eli. "I really don't want a big fuss, maybe a catered dinner in the party room on the roof?"

"It's a good opportunity to have everyone over who've invited you to their parties," I said.

"I can have a DJ, maybe a live band too, ugh, I don't want such a big deal," he said grimacing.

"Why don't you ask Carolyn Davies to come up with something, she's a great party planner, let her do all the work."

"I can do that, she's just a bit over the top, I'll tell her to keep it simple," he said.

I was lying on my stomach, naked, tanning at the lap pool on our balcony, I wanted to get an all over tan. Our patio was totally private, the building was built so that no one could see into each other's private space.

My cell phone pinged—a message from the security desk downstairs that Ms. Janet Dally was on her way up.

"Oh shit," I said, "what does she want now?"

"I'm not waiting around to see," said Eli.

She knocked loudly once and walked in the door. I hurriedly went to my room to throw on some clothes.

"Haile!" she called out, "you won't believe what happened to me."

"Be there in a sec," I said.

I put on a kaftan, brushed my hair, put on a sunhat, a bit of lipstick, mascara and rushed out breathless.

"No wonder you took forever," she said, "you are dressed for lunch on a yacht."

"What happened?" I said.

"You are not going to believe this," she said, annoyed, "I get an email from the condo board this morning, that they had a poop DNA match to my Buddy. I mean, come on, something is wrong with this story. I always pick up, always, what the fuck?"

"DNA doesn't lie," I said.

"This could be a set up," she said, "everyone hates me, they could have taken a sample out of the trash can after I had left the dog walk and said that it was from the ground."

"I don't think that the board would go to all that trouble," I said, "how much is the fine?"

"Two hundred and fifty dollars," she said, "I'm not going to pay it. They can sue me; this is a conspiracy."

"I'm almost glad that we don't have a dog anymore, the rules and regulations are becoming too much," I said.

"Is Eli here? Go get him, I want to get his take on this," she said.

"He has gone to the mall," I said.

"But his car is outside the door," she said.

"I'll go and check," I said, "this place is so big it's hard to keep tabs on everyone."

I walked to the back suite, "Eli!" I shouted loudly.

"Yes?" he said.

"Janet wants to talk to you."

"I'm in the shower," he said.

"I'll wait," she said, sitting down. "He can maybe explain to me how the board came up with this crap."

"Let's go downstairs and see if it's at all possible to pull a sample out of the doggy trash bins," I said, "don't forget that there are security cameras all over the place, so if anyone did something like that, it would be recorded."

"Oh right," she said, "the cameras."

We went down to the dog walk and above every trash can, where there were plastic baggies and wipes, was a video camera filming twenty-four seven.

A resident walking his dog said, "The DNA just confirms the fact that someone didn't pick up after their dog, everything is on the video anyway."

Janet got very quiet.

"You can always ask to see the video stamped on that date and time," he said.

She paid the fine to the condominium board and it was never mentioned again.

CHAPTER THIRTY-SIX:

JANNA

As it turned out, it was fun that Selena and I were at the hotel at the same time. I asked her which of the little towns were her favorite.

"I loved Avignon," she said, "we were too rushed on the tour, so I never got to see much, but it really has everything that I like, its quaint yet lively place full of culture and history and there is great shopping. I was dying to look at the clothing boutiques, but we didn't have enough time."

"We can go back there," I said, "it's only about an hour away, and I have a car. I know my way around because I have been there many times; would you like that?"

"I would love that!"

"Is today good?" I asked.

"I'm dressed and ready," she laughed.

We drove in my rented Mercedes to Avignon; the medieval walled town is set on the Rhone River. No visitor traffic is allowed inside the walls, so we drove to the parking garage closest to the main gate which opens onto the massive Popes Palace. There was a parade taking place, and we watched in awe as the soldiers dressed in medieval costumes threw their colorful flags up into the air, caught them with one hand then twirled them.

As we were about to leave, I suddenly felt dizzy; I tripped and fell, hitting my head on a large stone ledge.

"Oh my god!" Selena cried, looking at me sprawled out on the cobbled pavement with a blood gushing out of my forehead. In seconds a crowd of people had gathered around all offering to help, the Avignon Security Team arrived and promptly called for an ambulance. The chef from a nearby restaurant rushed out in his chef hat with paper towels and a chair for me to sit on while waiting for the ambulance to arrive and as soon as they did, the medics bandaged my head and took my vital signs. They put me in the ambulance and with Selena sat behind me in the back. They told me that they were transporting me to the closest hospital in Avignon. With sirens on, we descended slowly through the narrow, winding roads, leading out of the walled city and then headed to the emergency room at the Avignon Hospital Center.

No one spoke English and we didn't speak French, but the doctors knew what needed to be done; they took a cat scan of my head and sewed me up. Selena drove us back to St. Remy.

"I think the heat did me in," I said, "I was overcome with dizziness."

"You must take it easy for now," she said, "when you get back to the States you will have your stitches out. You just have to make sure that you are not concussed."

The rest of my time in St. Remy I spent convalescing in the garden at Mas des Carassins, reading a book. Jacques and Henri brought me all my meals to my room which I ate out on the patio. Selena rented a bicycle and most days she went cycling around the country roads and in the evenings, she would have dinner with me in my suite. I was very grateful to have her company.

"What do you do for a living?" I asked her.

"I'm a hairstylist," she said, then I realized how perfectly cut her spiked hairstyle was.

"Do you cut your own hair?" I asked.

"Yes," she laughed, "I didn't do such a good job, it's not very symmetrical. If you weren't in real estate, what would you have liked to do instead?"

"I actually have a teaching degree, but I never used it," I said, "Real estate is far more financially viable. I find it challenging and rewarding," I said.

"Do you ever regret not teaching," she asked.

"Oh no, I would have been a terrible teacher," I said, "I have no patience and I don't like children."

"Just as well you found that out before it was too late," she laughed.

She had a way of cocking her head while listening intently, she really made me feel that she was interested in everything I had to say.

Wednesday was market day and I felt well enough to go into town. If you didn't get into the center very early there wasn't a chance of finding a spot to park your car. The locals knew which regular food vendors would be there, so they did their fruit, vegetable, cheese, meat and fish shopping on that day. I had already filled my home with pottery, tablecloths, and paintings from previous visits to Provence, but Selena was excited to do some serious shopping. I was thankful that she was a fast shopper like me. She picked out T-shirts, some boho dresses, and a straw hat in lightning speed.

We found an Italian restaurant close to the central square and we chose to sit outdoors because it was such a lovely day—we each ordered a margherita pizza and when the waiter brought them to the table, we realized that one would have been sufficient to share. Selena confided in me that she was dreading going home to San Francisco.

"Sara will have moved out of the apartment, and it's going to be tough getting used to living on my own again," she said.

"I'm not looking forward to going back to my messy life either," I said.

"Is your relationship over with this guy?" she asked.

"I'm not sure," I said, "he seemed to be conflicted about leaving his kids, not so much his wife, but the family unit."

"It's often the case that when a married man has an affair they go back to their wives in the end. Do you agree?"

"I do, but I'm not giving up so easily," I said.

"Do you love him?" she asked.

"I love the thought of winning more," I laughed.

"You are terrible!" she said, "at least you are honest. How do you plan on keeping him?"

"Well, don't choke on your pizza," I said, "I'm going to use the oldest trick in the book."

"Tell me it's not what I think it is," she said, her eyes wide.

"I'm going to try and get pregnant."

"That's such a trap," she said, "you really play dirty."

"I'm forty-three, so it's not going to be easy. I've always wanted a child. After I get back, I'm going to ask my gynecologist for options I have to make me fertile."

"But what if you fall pregnant with his child and he still doesn't want a relationship? She said, "That would be more realistic don't you think?"

"I can do it on my own because I am financially stable," I explained, " but because he would be the father, I will make sure that he will have to support the child too. Then he would be forced to be a part of our lives."

"That sounds so conniving, don't you feel bad for his wife and three children?"

"Not at all," I said, "if he has sex with me, then he has to take the consequences. Not once has he asked me if I'm on birth control."

"You also have this harassment case hanging over you," she said.

"A big cloud over me," I said, "although this morning I got an email from my attorney, and she said that this is going to be hard to prove because there are no witnesses or no other complaints from other women."

"Will you still pursue this?"

"I'm thinking now that I may just settle for a fair cash amount, I don't have the energy to fight this if I am not going to win," I said, "I would rather put all my energy into pursuing James."

"Janna, after your bad fall you have to realize how fragile life is. Sometimes, its better not to always be right and try to win. Peace of mind is more important don't you agree?"

"You may be right," I said.

"Karma is a bitch, what goes around comes around, remember that," Selena added.

We were both flushed and giggling, the two bottles of wine contributed to our tipsy lunch.

We could barely make it up the hill back to the hotel and both of us collapsed on our beds in our rooms and fell asleep with our clothes on.

CHAPTER THIRTY-SEVEN:

ELI

I was driving to Miami Beach when I got a call from Clint Yarrow, my Private Investigator.

"Hey man, can you talk?" he asked.

"Yes, I'm driving," I said, "any news?"

"I have some interesting information. Firstly, Ms. Cooper is in Provence, France, in the town of Saint Remy, staying at a local hotel. My informant has befriended her and was able to get some confidential information for us," he said.

"You planted someone there?" I asked.

"Of course. I knew this woman would be the perfect one to gain her confidence. I put her up at the same hotel as Ms. Cooper and this is what she found out. Ms. Cooper is adamant to pursue James LaValle with the hope of him leaving his wife. She has indicated that she will do all that it takes including trying to fall pregnant by him."

"Oh no," I said.

"I have all the conversations taped. Most importantly she also said that she may be willing to drop your case because her attorney has advised her to, however, she will still try and get a cash settlement from you, so you won't be totally let you off the hook."

"Interesting," I said, "disturbing for Mr. LaValle but good for me."

"Here is another tidbit; Ms. Cooper had an accident in Avignon the other day, she slipped and hit her head on the ground and had to go to the nearby ER for stitches."

"You are kidding! Maybe she had some sense knocked into her," I said.

"My informant also told me that Ms. Cooper had complained about feeling dizzy prior to this fall. I believe Ms. Cooper will be back in the States in the next few days."

"Thank you, Clint, you did a great job as usual, let's talk soon."

I felt like a huge weight had been lifted off my shoulders. Kerry must have convinced Janna to drop the case. I felt responsible to warn Camilla what I had found out about Janna's plans to destroy her marriage. Even though Camilla had told me that she wasn't going to reconcile with her husband, she had to know what she was up against.

I felt that I could breathe easier and now felt optimistic to organize a party for my fiftieth birthday. I would call Carolyn, the party planner and tell her to plan the logistics. I told her that I wanted an elegant, fun affair with good food and great music. We would transform the rooftop into a stunning space. The view from the fortieth floor was spectacular with water views as far as the eye could see. I wanted tiki torches, white muslin tents and the ultimate island retreat. There was already suitable outdoor furniture there, but I wanted to bring in large lounging couches and hanging hammocks. Tropical flowers and white gardenias would be flown in for the occasion. If I was going to have a party, it had to be the best and I was now in the mood to celebrate.

"How big is the guest count?" Carolyn said.

"About one hundred," I said, "my secretary will send you the invitation list."

When I got home, I told Haile the good news.

"My PI told me that Cruella is dropping the lawsuit."

"How did that come about?" she said.

"He planted a spy at the hotel where she is staying in France and got the information that way."

"That's brilliant," she said.

"Another tidbit I found out was that Janna is serious about getting together with James, she even told this woman that she would resort to falling pregnant to trap him," I said.

"That's crazy," Haile said, "I would think that she was too old to conceive."

"I guess where there's a will, there's a way," I said.

I stretched out on the sofa, feeling happier than I had in weeks.

"I'm going to celebrate my birthday in style," I said.

"Great idea," she said, "invite everyone who is a part of your work and social life. Janna will get wind of it and realize that she is a pariah now."

I drove over to Camilla's house, her car was in the driveway, I rang the doorbell. The housekeeper spoke to me through the video cam.

"Is Miss Camilla home?" I asked, "this is Eli Selig."

"She is not home right now," she said.

I could hear Vinnie barking, then I heard Camilla call out, "Gabriella, it's OK, let him in," she said.

"Hi hon," she said giving me a hug.

She was dressed from the waist up, in a silk blouse, perfectly made-up and wearing pearl earrings, she also had on a pair of torn denim shorts.

"I had a video call with my attorney," she said explaining the weird attire.

"You still going through with the divorce?' I asked.

"Definitely," she said, "I'm not willing to carry on with this façade."

She asked the housekeeper to bring us tea and cookies on the patio.

"I heard from a reliable source that Janna is going to make a play for your husband," I said.

"She can have him," she said, "I bet he won't want her—that's his modus operandi, get the girl then dump her."

"How are the kids holding up?" I asked.

"All three of them are acting off the wall. They don't listen, have tantrums, they are acting out at school. The older two are in therapy," she said. "They don't want to go to James on the weekends, it's a mess."

"I'm having a birthday party in two weeks, will you come?"

"Are you inviting James?" she said.

"Yes, I have to."

"I'll come for you, I will put on my big girl pants and just suck it up," she said, "as long as the bitch won't come near the place."

"Are you kidding? Of course, she won't be there, she is my arch enemy too," I said.

Camilla took a sip of her green tea. "Eli, thank you for everything that you have done for me," she said. "I don't know what I would do without you."

She reached out and squeezed my hand, when I looked up, she had tears in her eyes.

"Everything will be alright in the end," I said, "it's just not the end yet."

CHAPTER THIRTY-EIGHT:

THE PARTY

Eli had not slept the night before the party. As he lay in bed he felt as if a heavy boulder was pressing on his chest, he couldn't breathe, he was sweating, and his heart was racing.

As the sun came up, panicking he got up and went to Haile.

"I am not feeling well," he said.

"What is the matter?" she said.

"It feels like I am having a heart attack."

"Have you ever felt like this before?" she asked.

"Not in a long time, but when I was younger."

"You are having a panic attack," then she said, "breath in through your nose slowly and out slowly through your mouth."

We did this together until I felt calmer.

"I can't go to my party," Eli said,

"I know how you feel," she said, "the more you calm down the better you will feel."

"I can't go," he said, "I am paralyzed."

"Should we cancel?"

"You go in my place," he said.

"Me? I can't, you know how socially inept I am."

"You have to do this for me. Tell them that I was held up in New York and because of the snowstorm, which is true, all the planes are all grounded."

"This will be very hard for me, but I will do it. You are my everything."

The top floor was transformed into an exotic lush paradise—all the senses were covered from heady floral infused perfume to the large containers of imported banana trees and the delicious aromas from the simmering food all combined with a trio playing the steel drums, made you feel like you had stepped onto a private tropical island.

The only thing that was missing was the birthday boy himself—a lavish party held without the host, Halie didn't know how she would address this.

She was dressed in a man's tuxedo, with her hair pulled back in a high ponytail and her face make up heavily applied to resemble and exotic cat, whiskers and all.

James LaValle was the first confused guest to approach her, "where is Eli? I want to wish him a happy birthday?"

"Eli, is held up in a snowstorm in New York," she said, "he can't get here."

"Well, that's a disaster," he said, "my soon to be ex will be devastated, she is his biggest fan."

Bizarre news spreads like a bad virus. Haile lost count of how many times she had to explain Eli's missing whereabouts."

"You should have canceled," they said.

"It was too late," she explained.

"Well, we may as well make the best of a party," they said.

Others said, "this is totally fucked up, if we had known we would have never come."

Everyone who was anyone in the Miami social scene was there, not because they really wanted to but because of the fear of missing out.

The food was served buffet style throughout the evening, so you could eat, drink, or have dessert whenever you felt like it.

Despite the missing VIP, when the live band started playing, there wasn't an empty space on the dance floor. This was an opportunity to show off one's best moves and fueled by the cocktails, this crowd did not disappoint. Hands in the air, higher and higher, butts vibrating, hips pulsating, expressionless faces too cool to make eye contact; everyone having fun without showing it.

Haile may have been physically present, but she felt like she was observing the scene from another planet. Camilla came up to her.

"I'm Camilla La Valle," she said, "I have been dying to meet you.

"I've heard a lot of good things about you from Eli," Haile said.

"This really sucks for Eli. I am so worried about him; he hasn't been himself lately, we are very close, you know. Is the snowstorm an excuse?" she asked looking intently into Haile's eyes.

Haile slowly nodded and Camilla took her hand and squeezed it.

"I thought so," she said, "I'm feeling very anxious myself, this is the first time that I have been to a social gathering on my own. My estranged husband is here acting like he doesn't have a care in the world."

"Eli told me what you are going through, it's tough especially in this small town where everyone knows your business," said Haile.

"The crazy thing is that you live with someone, love them and then when it's over you become like strangers, as if the whole relationship was just an illusion."

Camilla stiffened and a look of horror came over her face, "What the fuck is she doing here? I thought she wasn't invited," she said.

Haile turned towards Camilla's gaze. Janna Cooper came strutting through the rooftop door.

"How she get in?" Haile said, "Eli left specific instructions for security not to let anyone in who wasn't on the guest list."

Haile strode towards Janna, "What are you doing here?" she asked, "you are not invited."

"I'm well aware of that fact," she said, "I came to give Eli a birthday surprise."

"He isn't here," Haile said.

"Oh, come on," she said, "who are you to tell me that your brother isn't here."

"He isn't. He couldn't make it."

'I wasn't born yesterday," she scoffed, "I'm not going to make a scene. I just wanted to tell him in person that I am dropping the lawsuit, it's my birthday gift to him."

"This is not the time or place," Haile said.

"You may be Eli's sister," she said taking a glass of champagne off a tray, "but he can't think much of you, he sure keeps you hidden out of sight."

As soon as she walked away Camilla said, "I hate that woman, she has destroyed my life. I am going to leave."

"Don't go, Camilla," Haile said, "you take the high road, don't give her the power to make you leave."

Haile watched as Janna cornered James who was visibly unnerved; while she was ranting, he ran his fingers through his hair nervously, clearing his throat. Whatever she was saying did not look good.

Carolyn, the party planner came up to Haile and whispered that she should make an announcement explaining the reason why Eli was missing in action and thank the guests for coming.

Haile agreed.

"I'll tell the master of ceremonies to ask everyone to come out on the landing and you can say a few words. A good place is by the railing overlooking the ocean," she said.

It was a perfect night; a new moon illuminated the water, and you could hear the rhythm of the waves lapping below. The guests formed a half circle around Haile, Camilla stood to her left and James to the right, keeping a safe distance from each other.

Haile tapped on her glass with a fork and said, "Can you all hear me? I want to welcome each and every one of you and to apologize that the birthday boy for no fault of his own unfortunately could not be here tonight. He is in New York City on business and as you all know all flights were cancelled due to the massive snowstorm. He was meant to fly back to Miami last night and is very disappointed that he couldn't be here, in the meantime.."

Her voice trailed off as she saw at the corner of her eye, Janna clutching the hem of her long dress attempting to climb up on the ledge overlooking the beach.

"Hey guys," she said teetering in her high heels, holding her phone with her one hand,

"Pay no attention to me, I just want to take a photo of this hysterical, I mean historical moment for my memory bank." She was obviously drunk and slurring her words.

"Get down from there," Haile commanded.

She rocked backwards and you could hear a collective gasp, hands grabbed desperately at her dress trying to pull her forward.

"What the fuck are you doing?" someone yelled.

Haile reached out in the panic trying to grab Janna's ankles, but it was too late.

In a split second, she lost her balance and in a slow-motion sequence fell backwards and then hurtled down towards the ground. We were too high up to hear the thump as she hit the ground. Everyone pushed forward, looking over the railing as her body lay sprawled down below. The band started playing, unaware of the commotion.

"Celebrate good times, come on!" They sang, trailing off when they realized that something bad had happened.

A few of the guests tried going downstairs but the elevators were taking too long. By the time Haile got down, the paramedics had already arrived followed by firetrucks and the police. Red lights flashing, sirens howling, men in uniform wheeling a gurney through to the beach side.

They placed a screen around the lifeless body but the neighbors hanging over their balconies had a clear view of what was going on below. The immediate rumor was a suicide, she was a jilted lover, a guest of the wild party on the roof and she took her own life. Channel seven news almost immediately had a helicopter surveying the scene.

The police stood guard at the door to the rooftop and gave orders that no one was to leave the party before being interviewed. They set up a table with chairs and called each guest one at a time to validate their identification, contact information and answer a slew of questions. This had a sobering effect on all the previous gaiety.

They repeated the same questions. Why did she climb up? How did she lose her balance? Was she drunk? Exactly how did she fall? Why was she taking a photo?

Everyone had the same answers, no one could give a plausible reason why this beautiful young woman would do something so irresponsible and stupid.

Once the police were done with the interviews everyone was allowed to leave except Haile.

No one noticed that Haile was led up to her apartment and questioned for a few hours. The detectives took a particularly long look at her ID and her passport. Eli was questioned too and there seemed to be a confusion over the papers.

The police took away all the security video cameras and after going through them many times, they gave a full report to the board that Janna Cooper's demise was the result of an accidental death. No foul play suspected. A full autopsy was in progress to see if alcohol or narcotics played a part.

IN CONCLUSION

For days after the 'incident' the chatter around Miami Beach was very loud, if they weren't there, everyone knew someone who was there.

"Definitely suicide," some said, "she told my cousin that she was going to jump."

Others reported, "I saw her take mushrooms in the bathroom, and she thought she was Superwoman."

The closest to the truth was, "she was having an affair with James La Valle, and she jumped because he wanted to go back to his wife."

Soon all the gossip stopped, and everyone went back to worrying about their own lives.

A few days went by when Eli asked Camilla to meet him at a designated deserted parking lot just on the edge of town. He drove an unremarkable car, parked next to hers and hopped into the passenger seat.

"You know that I was at my birthday party?" he said.

"You were hiding behind the bushes?" she laughed.

"Look at me," he said, "I am very serious, I have a dark secret to tell you. I don't have a sister."

"She's your girlfriend?" Camilla asked.

"Haile is me and I am Haile. We are the same person."

"I don't understand," she said.

"The security cameras did not show that," he said, "the police went over them with a fine-tooth comb."

"Cam, don't be shocked, but I live a double life."

"A double life?"

"I will tell you something that I have never told a soul and you must promise never to tell anyone."

"OK," she said.

The early dawn light cast shadows on their faces, they reached for each other's hands, clasped then together as if to you confirm that this was not a dream. Coffee lovers started pulling up in their cars to the parking lot, then standing in line at the Cuban restaurant window to get their early morning Cortadito shot of coffee before heading out to work.

Eli bent forward, cleared his throat and began explaining, "When I was a little boy, I was sexually abused by my father, the only way that I knew how to cope was to split myself in two—Haile who took the brunt of the suffering and then me, Eli, who did not."

"That is so fucked up," she said, "your father sexually abused you, his son?"

"Yes. The only way survived was by switching myself into someone else, a girl. I did this then and I still do it now. I have an alter ego, Haile, and when I come home, I transform myself physically and mentally—it is the only time that I feel at peace."

"You have fooled everyone, you look like a woman, you act and speak like one," Camilla said.

"It has taken me many years to perfect. Every detail has been thought of, even my name. As you know I am Eliah Selig and if you spell that backwards it is Haile Giles, get it?" Eli said.

"I don't know what to say?" she said, "It's obviously a mental by-product of what you went through as a kid. Who am I to judge? Everyone has always told me how beautiful your sister is, weird, but stunning."

"It's not uncommon for abuse victims to split their personalities for survival. This had been very tough for me. I have been living a double life and it's taken its toll," Eli said.

"I have always thought of you as kind of androgynous, you are soft and feminine as well as masculine, it's so crazy. The other day when I touched your hand it was so smooth," she said. "Since I was seven years old, my life unraveled. I was at my lowest ebb when we went on a family cruise and it was there that I made up an imaginary friend, a girl, whom I called Haile, and she became my savior."

"I feel so bad for you," Camilla said, tearing up.

"After Janna's accident, after interviewing me, the police scrutinized my true identity on my picture ID. They saw that my name was male, Eliah Helig, yet I was dressed as a female. They were confused and I had to tell them that I dress and present myself as a woman at well. They asked me if I was transgender and I had to explain that I identify as male, but I dress as a female, closer to a transvestite."

"It's so complicated," she said.

"After they did a background check on me, they seemed satisfied," he said, "but there is something else that I have to confess to you. When Janna was about to fall over the ledge, instead of pulling her in, I think that I pushed her."

"I can understand why you do that?"

"There is something else," Eli said, "when Janna was about to fall over the ledge, instead of pulling her in, I pushed her—that's what I think I did."

"You think, you don't know?" she said.

"The security videos were investigated thoroughly, the report states it was an accident, there was no evidence of any foul play."

"Surely that shows you that you didn't do it."

"I wanted to that is all I remember, everything happened to fast."

"Why are you telling this?"

"Because I trust you, I know what you have been through and really Cami you are the first person that I have ever had feelings for," he said.

"Are you ever going to be a whole person?"

"I have been thinking about that a lot lately, I am ready to incorporate Haile into me and my goal through further treatment is to meld the two person-alities together."

"We can help each other heal," she said, "I have had not been happy for a long time."

"One more thing the detective's told me. The report from Janna's autopsy states that she was in the first weeks of pregnancy."

"Do you think that James was the father?"

"I do know that she was trying to trap him that way."

"It's so sad," she said.

"Yes," Eli said

They kissed, very lightly and very softly. There were no sparks or fireworks, just a feeling of coming home.

Camilla was awarded the newly built house on the Golden Beach as part of the divorce settlement; she, the children, Eli and Vinnie the dog, moved in together—and on the rare occasion Haile comes to visit.